A Simple Child

by Louise Michell

DORRANCE
PUBLISHING CO
EST 1920
PITTSBURGH, PENNSYLVANIA 15238

Dorrance Publishing Co
585 Alpha Drive
Pittsburgh, PA 15238
Visit our website at www.dorrancebookstore.com

ISBN: 978-1-4809-8939-9
eISBN: 978-1-4809-8913-9

A Simple Child is dedicated to all those with Down syndrome and the wonderful people who care for them.

Acknowledgments

To Paula and Rachel, my wonderful sisters
To my Jo and her book club, for their feedback and comments
To Emma, who nearly read it, Alice who will read it and Vicky who did read it!

To Gail and Jo, without whom this book would not have got off the ground.
To Tyrrell and Sian, for their love and support
To Hazel, for her help and advice in getting going

And of course to Michael……..

Between the realms of hopelessness and purpose, a simple child must wend his trustful way.

Can ever light be brought unto the unknowing mind of the simple child, who spends his life at play?

But, we can learn a message from his heart, and he has something wonderful to give.

For if we all can see the innocence of his eyes, his humbleness and joy, the gift to live.

ILS 1965

1

George

I still remember what it is to anticipate. To dream of something bigger than you can imagine, yet have no knowledge of it. Until the moment it happens. And then, it cannot be put back. It is with you forever.

And so it was that night, a night etched into my childhood memory, a black night, filled with foreboding. The fickle stars and moon had retreated, hidden by gathering storm clouds, and the stifling air gave a feeling of unsought tension. It was that life-changing night that I would never forget, not even to this day, and the consequences of what happened then will stay with us forever.

Lightening, a sudden flash. Then, a pause, until a distant rumble of thunder sounded, like a demon dog growling, hungry and impatient. It seemed as though our world was anxiously on hold, and the Gods were angry, fighting and squabbling in the midnight sky. Waiting, waiting… I still cannot describe that anticipation, even though I am now a man, it is a childish feeling etched into my psyche, more so because of what it was about to bring.

"What's happening?" a tiny voice whispered.

My brother and I were hiding in a dank and musty corridor, trying to make sense of the noises seeping out from the nearby bedroom. There were human voices, one loud and purposeful, others muffled, but I could also make out the deep tones of our father, nervously mumbling. Suddenly, there came piercing screams that made my brother sob.

"Shush," I whispered, "they'll hear us"

"Push… Push…" a rather stern female voice commanded, its tone urging, cajoling. "Come on, nearly there!"

There came more swallowed screams, and then… Nothing.

"What's happening?" my brother asked again, this time softly and with even more terror in his voice.

"I don't know. I think Mother's ill," I mumbled. "Something's wrong."

"What do you mean?"

"Shush," I breathed.

Silence, then low murmurings, muffled voices stretching our hearing to its limits. I thought I could hear my mother sobbing, and that awful sound seemed to drive an icy stake through my thumping heart, making me shiver.

"Is it alright? What's happening?" I could just make out my mother's shaky voice.

And then, seemingly oblivious to all its audience, a weak cry, like a kitten mewing, slowly getting louder and stronger.

"There, it's all okay," said my father, the relief obvious. Then, there was a pause, unwelcomed and worrying.

"Where are you taking him?" gasped my mother.

"Just getting the doctor to have a look, nothing to worry about."

More murmurings.

I didn't understand. I knew both my brother and I longed to run into the room and find our mother, but we were both too terrified to move.

"What are you two doing here? Come on, back to bed, right now!"

Aunt Amelia dragged us both by the backs of our well-worn pyjamas and shooed us into our small bedroom. Two rickety beds sat side by side with precious little room to move between them; an ancient chest of drawers that wobbled and squeaked every time it was opened, and an old chair, rescued from a rubbish dump, graced our tiny dormitory. For my brother and I, it was a small oasis, a place where mother would come and read us bedtime stories, the same ones over and over, as our library was small and meager. The well-worn pages of *The Water Babies* and *The Wind in the Willows* were so often a comfort before the long dark hours of sleep. And, it was a comfort that we had each other in that tiny room, although I would never let on to my brother that I needed him in any way. I was too proud for that.

But I do remember the feeling of his presence somehow making life easier. This was especially true since Aunt Amelia had arrived the day before, flustered and overbearing, her black attire with never a splash of colour and her high-pitched voice, constantly scolding.

"George, Arthur… Go to sleep! I don't want to catch you out of bed again!"

She left us in the pitch darkness, my brother shaking, and my own senses frozen like a trapped rabbit.

Another flash of lightening and rumble of thunder made my young brother jump, then shiver and whimper.

"What's happening? I want Mother"

"She can't come now, Artie. Don't worry; it'll be alright." I tried to sound reassuring, but I suspect my voice sounded squeaky and upset too.

I looked around the gloomy room, my eyes now adapted to the darkness. The tattered curtains fluttered as the wind forced its way through the cracks in the frame and did nothing to block the flashes of lightening. The old carpet looked so tired, its pattern faded and threadbare. I tried to focus on staying calm, but my mind was a jumble, and I was torn between running off again to mother's bedroom, or staying with little Artie. At that time, being the eldest and only eight years old, I knew I had to be strong. I was a child, yet in my mind, I can still recall that I experienced a dichotomy of thought that pulled me away from childishness and childish thoughts and told me to be a man. Artie, at four years old, was quite definitely only a child, and although it was sometimes irritating, I felt responsible for him, especially with Aunt Amelia around. I tried not to be afraid of her, and sometimes, she could almost show warmth and, dare I say it, even love. But those breaks in her own clouds were few and far between.

There was now something much more important to think about. Why did mother sound so distraught? Did we have a baby brother or sister? What would happen to us now? I felt Artie shiver again, so I put my arm around him, and he snuggled gratefully against me, both of us squashed into my bed for comfort.

We were left there, holding each other tightly, and somehow, with the storm crashing around outside like a demented ogre, both of us fell into a deep sleep.

That was what I remember of the birth of my little brother. We didn't see him, or Mother for some weeks after that stormy episode. Aunt Amelia came into us each morning and made us wash and dress quickly in the chill bathroom, and then gave us breakfast and put us outside into the back yard to play until lunchtime, like unwanted pups.

We lived in a tiny, terraced house on the outskirts of a bustling town. My overriding memories were of the colours grey and brown. The street was brown, with faded red brick buildings that only occasionally attempted to be house proud. It was though we lived in a sepia photograph. And then there was the greyness, grey clouds and grey clothes on grey people. I'm sure there must have been colour, no doubt the odd floral apron or brightly coloured hat on a special occasion, but somehow, it did not penetrate into my awareness.

There was little money in those days, and the people who lived in our street tended to keep to themselves, except when there was gossip to be had. No one passed by much, and we rarely spoke to anyone. We were drilled with that adage ringing in our ears that "children should be seen and not heard."

But no one saw us, so who could possibly hear us?

The air of downtrodden resignation that had slowly descended after the war was now a true presence in our little community. Although there had been great camaraderie during those desperate years of conflict, it seemed to have dissipated, and the common man was now struggling to keep body and soul together. He was free, but still reeling at the cost. Rationing continued, and grief, at first suppressed by the elation of having won the war, started to permeate.

Every family had lost something or someone. I remember overhearing a rare conversation between my mother and a neighbour about a poor woman who had lost her husband and two brothers over the six years of conflict.

"Poor Mavis," the woman had said to my mother as she ventured out to the shops one day, holding tightly to Artie's hand and trying to escape the encounter. "Lost them all within the space of a week – never seen the telegram boy so busy, dreadful it was."

"Is that the boy with the bicycle? I'd love one like that."

"Shush, dear." My mother tried to whisk us away, while nodding sympathetically at the woman.

"Who is Mavis?" asked Artie.

"Quiet, dear, you know you shouldn't talk when adults are talking."

Children were indeed still seen and not heard; fathers ruled households, and no one spoke of difficult or dangerous subjects. There was, I suppose, a strong sense of family, of stiff upper lip, and in our particular case, this culminated in Aunt Amelia appearing whenever there was trouble. She had never married, and some spoke of her having had a broken heart. She occasionally came to stay on high days or holidays, but always if Mother needed help. I don't know how she felt about Artie and me. Perhaps she was jealous of Mother, as she had no children of her own. She had little compassion from what I could discern, but she clearly had a strong sense of right and wrong when it came to family. I couldn't tell you how old she was then. Her short, severe hair was iron grey. Her face, perpetually unhappy, looked younger somehow, as if time had stood still for her, and she had been caught in its folly. I had an overwhelming sense of a soul trapped in another epoch, another time and another place, as if she didn't want to be here at all. She frightened me, but I realised I also felt a little sorry for her.

My father tended to pay more attention to his elder sister's pontifications than my mother's gentle word. This irritated me, and sometimes, I wanted to shout at him to stand up for Mother, who hated us to be treated harshly. Aunt Amelia's standard practice was to shoo Artie and I into the back yard whenever she could, to get us out of her hair. The yard was a small and dingy place, surrounded by walls that looked as if they could crumble on a whim. There was little to do there, but Artie always had an imaginary game for us to play, and although even then I thought myself too old for such nonsense, those games were strangely comforting. At that moment, they took my mind off what we had inadvertently witnessed with Mother on that dreadful night.

"You can be a wizard, and I'll be the magic!" cried Artie, draping an old piece of cloth about his shoulders as though he were a conjuror. "Magic me a wand," he commanded

I remember I picked up a bit of discarded piping and handed it to him with a flourish.

"There," I said, ducking as he wafted it about his head.

"I am magic, and I can see through the sky!" He beamed.

Artie often told me of another place, far above our heads, a place that existed 'through' the sky, where he was able to communicate with all sorts of creatures and beings.

"Who is there today?" I asked, pretending to be interested.

"Tibbles!" he cried.

Tibbles had been the cat from the vicarage, it's nine lives extinguished when it had been run over in the street right outside our house by Mr. Jacob's delivery van. This was much to the distress of his owner, the vicar's wife, who had to be given tea and sympathy by my mother, one of the few times we had entertained anyone, and under rather unfortunate circumstances. Artie, who had befriended the cat when it had jumped into our yard in search of tidbits, had been upset but pragmatic at the loss. This was because, as it transpired, he refused to believe the cat was dead. I must say, it had looked pretty lifeless to me after the van had trundled away.

"Tibbles is lying in his favorite spot near the fire!" Artie exclaimed. "And he says he knows what's for tea!"

"That's good," I humoured Artie. He loved it when I went along with his make-believe, and sometimes it was quite amusing.

"It's kippers!" he exclaimed.

"It's always kippers!" I said.

"Boys, time for tea."

Aunt Amelia was at the back door.

"Its kippers," she pronounced in her usual, definitive way.

I grinned. *Artie must have amazing powers,* I thought, *or just a rather good sense of smell!*

One day, as the air was getting slightly warmer and the days longer, my Aunt Amelia appeared on the stairs in her long black coat with her bags packed.

"Your Mother will look after you now," she announced, and then she was gone with a swish of her coat, until all we could see was her tiny figure disappearing down the hill towards the station. It was as though a cloud had lifted and dissipated in the wind, leaving fresher, brighter air.

"Come in, boys!"

We rejoiced at the familiar voice of our Mother, yet when we listened closely, she sounded different. Something had changed irreparably, and both my brother and I could sense it.

"Come in! Tea is ready."

We approached gingerly, and everything seemed normal and in its place. The old kitchen table stood firmly in the middle of the small parlour. The four chairs were placed exactly as they always had been, and there, as usual, was the photograph of Mother and Father's wedding in its silver frame watching us from the mantelpiece. But something new had arrived, inserted into our world with no announcement, no pomp or ceremony.

There, in the corner of the room, was a little basket with a tiny form, wrapped up in blankets and making no sound.

"What's this?" asked Artie?

"This is Isaac, your new brother."

"Can I play with him?"

"No, dear. He's very tiny and needs to sleep a lot."

"Well, can I at least see him?"

"Not yet, dear."

I was silent, unusual for me, because I had caught a glimpse of Isaac, in amongst all the blankets and fresh muslin, and he was Chinese.

I didn't really understand much about where babies came from at that time, but I knew that there was often a family likeness. "Oh, hasn't he got his father's chin?" or "He looks just like his mother when he smiles!" so I knew that this wasn't my brother, well not my proper brother. I racked my brains about Chinese people, but I could only think of the Chinese sailor who had lived three doors down. He had left for sea many months before. I was terrified. What was happening to our family? Where had Isaac come from?

I hadn't seen Father for days now, and whenever he did appear, he looked exhausted. There were grey rings under his usually bright green eyes, and his hair, fair and wavy, lacked luster and hung limply at his collar, desperately in need of a good barber. I knew he worked very hard at the factory, but before Isaac arrived, he had always played with us for at least five lively minutes in the yard before bedtime.

My mind turned over and over. What sort of a name was Isaac? It wasn't Chinese, so where did it come from? Did we have any uncles or cousins called Isaac? I had been named after my father as the first-born, and I was proud to be called George. My brother had been named after my Uncle Arthur, who had perished in the Great War. Father had often regaled us with tales of his strength and fortitude, and how he was such a hero to go to war. But a bit like fishing stories, I suspected the truth had been much exaggerated. My brother was known as Artie, mainly because I couldn't say Arthur properly when he was born, but also because it was a diminutive, just like my small brother. All this was accepted, and we knew the roots of our family. But who was Isaac?

After tea, Mother took us upstairs to wash and get ready for bed carrying Isaac in his basket. He hardly stirred, and she made sure he was well out of view of Artie and me as we changed.

This routine continued for a few weeks. The house was the same: the same cracks in the ceiling in our bedroom; the same creak and groan of the floor-boards when we walked across the landing, even the same large spider's web tucked into a high corner of the dingy little bathroom; but nothing felt the same. Father, usually present in the early mornings and back for tea each night to see us, was no longer present for breakfasts or bath times, and Mother, head permanently bowed, carried the basket wherever she went. There were few visitors to our house. The doctor, however, appeared on more than one occasion when father was home, and we could hear raised voices whenever he came.

"You know the doctor's right dear, he would be better off."

"No, he's not going anywhere. We'll manage"

A few weeks later, Mother had gone to lie down in the afternoon and had taken Isaac with her. Artie wanted to play his make-believe games again in the yard, but I wanted to see what was really in the basket.

I tiptoed into Mother's room and crept quietly to the cradle. I gently peeled back the muslin that covered the basket and looked inside. I was surprised to see a round face peering out at me. Isaac smiled a crinkly sort of smile. He still looked like a Chinese baby, but different. He made some little cooing sounds, but didn't move very much. I had seen a couple of six-month-old babies before. Mrs. Downside had paraded Baby Henry when he was half a year old at the school fete, sat up in his Silver Cross pram, and she boasted about how he could coo and chortle and grab at you with chubby fingers, but Isaac was just very quiet. He looked quite sweet really, but I still couldn't believe he could be my brother.

"George!"

My mother startled me.

"Be careful."

"I won't hurt him Mother," I said. "Is he really my brother? He looks Chinese."

"He's a Mongol," my mother whispered, slightly choking on the words.

"What's that?" I asked.

"He's just a bit different from us, that's all. He wasn't made quite right. But he is your brother. You know that Artie's got red hair, and you've got blond hair? Well, it's a bit like that. He's always going to be slower than you, and he'll always stay at home and not go out to school or work or anything, but he's ours, and we love him"

"I love him too," I said, trying to be brave and not quite sure if I meant it, but I knew in that moment that I felt incredibly protective of this little being.

My father left.

My mother said it was to go south to find work, but I didn't believe her.

She said we needed more money now that we had an extra mouth to feed, but I didn't see how that was true. Isaac hardly ate anything and still suckled slowly at my mother's breast. Artie and I were sent to a local school run by the church.

We weren't really churchgoers, but it wasn't looked upon well if a family didn't attend, so we tried to go to the services on Sundays as often as we could. Mother stopped going altogether once Isaac was born, but a kindly Scottish neighbour called for Artie and I every week and pushed a polished penny into each of our hands for the collection. Going to church meant we were able to go to the church school. This was important for mother and saved us having to travel miles to get our education.

Our kindly neighbour, Mrs. Joy, didn't have children of her own and was very supportive of mother when Isaac was born. She must have been in her seventies and walked with a stick. Her husband had died many years before.

My father used to say she had a well lived in face, but her eyes shone with compassion, and she was always helping someone or other. There would be a pie for a recently bereaved parishioner, or flower arranging for the church, babysitting, knitting socks for the poor, and many other unseen kindnesses. I don't think we noticed her much either; it was if she had always been there, like a well-worn armchair or a favorite picture. She had a wry sense of humor, and wasn't averse to poking fun at the rather stuffy canon who would sometimes take the services in the little parish church.

I remember the starkness of the church, its huge stained-glass windows belying the austerity below, the hard, slippery pews, impossible to sit still on; many parishioners turning and tutting at Artie, who seemed to have ants in his pants every Sunday morning. I remember the creaky old organ, played bravely by a stalwart of the parish, pumping her feet on the pedals as if her life depended on it.

The church school was strict, but fair, and the teachers genuinely tried to improve the lives of the children who attended. The headmaster was a big bear of a man and came from the Welsh valleys. He had created a great reputation for music and football for the little primary school. I loved both, but Artie wasn't so keen.

Often, Artie didn't want to go to school, as he found it hard to concentrate in class, so I had to make sure he walked with me, and that I deposited him promptly each morning at the classroom door. It wasn't far to walk there, but we both felt worried about leaving Mother on her own with Isaac. The boys at the school were pretty rough, and often, we would come home with bloodied noses or scraped knees. Most of the time, we were able to hold our own, but there were often taunts about our father.

One day, a couple of boys sidled over to us as we trudged back home along the dusty path, kicking at stones and dragging our feet.

"Where's he gone then, your Dad? He's left hasn't he, probably got a fancy woman," squeaked one rather fat and grubby boy.

"No, he hasn't!" yelled Artie and pushed the boy. I'm sure Artie had no idea what was meant by a "fancy woman," but I was pretty sure it meant something bad.

The boy went to strike, but I was too quick for him and knocked him to the ground, then cuffed his friend who tried to punch me in the back.

"My father's getting more money for us and our new brother!" yelled Artie, hiding behind me. The boy stood up with tears in his eyes.

"Gonna tell my Dad 'bout you! he'll floor yer when he finds out you hit me."

The boy and his friend left, sniveling, while I stood and stared at their disappearing backs. I wasn't worried by their empty threats. I wasn't sure the boy even had a dad of his own. We continued our homeward journey, Artie kicking at the stones along the way.

"What's a fancy woman?" he asked me.

"Don't worry about that," I said.

"But they're always saying bad things about father. Where's he gone anyway?"

"Like we said, he's getting more money for Mother and Isaac. He'll be back before you know it, you'll see."

But I didn't believe myself, not really, not anymore. At first, I thought he might return, but I could sense from Mother that, apart from sending money, there was little or no communication between them. As we walked on down the path, I tried to distract Artie and make him forget about the fight we'd just had with the fat boy and his grubby little mate.

Unfortunately, we had not gone unnoticed.

A bigger boy and some of his pals who had witnessed the altercation came over to us as we tried to hurry home.

"Where's this brother of yours then? We haven't seen him. Bet he doesn't exist!" he chirped as they danced around Artie and I, hampering our escape.

"Does too," I said.

"Come on then, show us!" he grinned, front tooth missing and the beginnings of fluff on his upper lip.

Before I could do anything, the gang of boys had followed us all the way home and pushed their way into the backyard door as we took off our shoes.

"Mother, it's alright. They've just come to see Isaac," I said matter-of-factly, trying to disguise what I was feeling.

Mother looked terrified.

"I'm not sure that's a good idea," she whispered, her eyes wide with fear.

"Come on, Missus. We love babies, we won't hurt him," said the big boy. He smiled sweetly, camouflaging his true intention.

"Please" I said, not wanting to be shown up in front of these lads.

Mother walked slowly and hesitantly across the room and picked Isaac out of his cot and brought him towards the eager group of boys.

"His name's Isaac."

The boys just stared. There were a few stifled giggles and then the boys left.

Mother sat quietly cradling Isaac, and I pulled Artie back into the kitchen.

"What's wrong with Isaac?" Artie whispered.

"He's a bit slow, that's all," I said.

"But he looks different, and Mother is always sad, and Father is never here! I wish he hadn't come."

"Don't say that. He's our brother, like I'm your brother, and we have to look after each other."

"I guess… Can I punch boys who make fun of him, like you do for me?"

"One day," I said. "Now, we'd better get washed for tea."

"Are you the man of the house now?"

"I guess."

I suppose I did guess that now. At the ripe old age of nine, I was no longer a child.

Our lives changed forever, and we started on a new journey together, just the four of us. Isaac was not like any other baby that I had ever known (in my vast experience). He was so quiet and undemanding. However, he took up all of my mother's emotional energy, as she fretted and worried about how he was going to cope in such a hostile world outside. Artie and I had to be good. When normally we would have fought or argued, we stopped. When normally we would have squabbled over a piece of cake or a toy, we didn't. It seemed stupid to fight when Mother was so vulnerable, so we didn't. Not that that meant we didn't want to, but usually we managed to hold our emotions in check and get on with helping Mother. Instinctively, we knew that we were less important.

There was a lot to do.

Isaac needed watching or feeding or changing for much longer than a normal baby. The routine, lack of support, and monotony of a child that was persistently just a baby, tired Mother out. And so Artie and I learned to do simple chores, like basic cooking. We learned to clear and wash the plates, bring in the coal, and to run errands. I suppose that out of necessity, I must have become worldly wise. I was more suspicious and skeptical of people's motives than Artie, and I learned to be minimalist in my conversation with strangers. Artie was better at trusting people. Sometimes he was right, and sometimes he was wrong, but between us, we built an emotional barricade for our mother that attempted to absorb the insults and innuendos that the outside world sent our way.

Mother spent most of her time indoors. Those waggling, idle tongues on our street called her a recluse, and rumors spread about her mental state. I caught a bit of the gossip now and again but kept my head down. We had one true friend, Mrs. Joy, who popped in when she could and seemed to produce stews and pies whenever they were needed. We didn't notice that she'd been in the house, save for some lovely aroma wafting from the kitchen. Mother absorbed these practical gifts with little emotion. It was as if she had nothing left to give, not even simple thanks, but Mrs. Joy's quiet interventions clearly helped her, and came without condition. I hoped that Mother was happy, but a part of her life had disappeared when Isaac arrived. I knew she loved Isaac and didn't want to change him in any way, as it was plain to see the joy that he brought her just by being.

But she had sacrificed her marriage and social world to care for this vulnerable, misunderstood little bundle. Even she herself didn't really understand why the world should be so hostile and why she should feel so ashamed. This world that destroyed people with its ignorance and judgments was the world we had been plunged into.

Isaac had a funny face, which would crinkle easily into a smile, and each of us would sit for hours playing simple games with him, over and over. He was a bit cross-eyed too, which gave him a quizzical look. He was slow to learn, but every now and again, he would master a new task or a new word that would bring smiles to all of us. He became the centre of our tiny universe. It would take hours of repetition and frustration and sometimes tears.

"Look, Isaac has just learned how to hold a spoon!" squealed Artie.

Simple milestones became cause for great celebration, usually in the form of us boys jigging around the room. This antic made Isaac laugh, so we did it even more. Isaac finally learned to walk at four years old. Artie and I were summoned into the small parlour to witness the event.

"Just look at your brother!" Mother said admiringly.

Isaac, who had sat on the floor quite happily for most of his life, was suddenly tottering around, then sitting with a big thud on his padded bottom! We all giggled, and Artie ran over to hug Isaac who beamed as though he knew he had achieved something special.

Father wasn't there to see it.

He sent money, but we rarely saw him.

I'd overheard some of the neighbours talking, gossiping again about father having a "fancy piece" down south.

Once again, I presumed that meant another woman, but I wasn't sure, and I didn't care to dwell on it.

In spite of all this, Mother managed to make ends meet, so we carried on with our lives, not daring to talk about father or money.

By the next winter, Mother could not venture beyond the house at all, so Artie and I took Isaac outside for a bit of fresh air when it was possible. As the days got longer, we got bolder, and after a while, we started to walk him down the road into the village. We would pick a time when there wouldn't be too many eyes watching us. As I remember these times, it seemed that Mrs. Joy was always there in the background, like some sort of guardian angel.

On one occasion, our courage rather overtaking us, we went into the post office to get some stamps, and Artie and Isaac and I had to stand in a queue. Tiny Isaac was quite boisterous that day and was in a jovial mood. He was still small and stood little more than hip-high. He loved tickling people and often tried to tickle us if we were near enough. In the queue, I let go of Isaac's hand for just a second, unaware that he could reach the person in front. He duly started to tickle them! The woman spun round and looked straight at... Mrs. Joy! How she had arrived in that spot at that moment, I have no idea, but the victim of the tickle glared at her and muttered "Well, I never!"

Mrs. Joy just smiled benignly, seemingly oblivious. Artie, who had seen exactly what had happened, was almost bent double with silent giggling. I managed to usher both Isaac and Artie back into the street, and we grabbed Isaac's hands and marched him away. We never did get our stamps!

Isaac loved his food. And he loved feeding other people. To coax him to eat when he was very young, Artie and I had always played "aeroplanes," a game to get Isaac to take food from us off a spoon. Eventually, Isaac learned how to hold a spoon himself and would play aeroplanes with us, digging his spoon in some food and whizzing it round in the air until it arrived at an open mouth – usually Artie's!

One day, we both came home from school to find Isaac sitting in front of our old black and white television set, trying to feed the newscaster! The man reading the news didn't seem at all bothered as Isaac shoveled his laden spoon at him, and Artie and I laughed and laughed. Isaac just carried on regardless.

Time marched on, bad memories faded and coping with day-to-day living took over each waking moment. We did what needed to be done. We didn't think too much about it; we just got on with it.

I was now 14 and had passed my eleven plus, enabling me to go to the local grammar school. I had always been quite good at sums and English, and since father had left, I read a lot. I realised that reading and studying hard was the only way I could be the man of the house. I needed to "know things."

Artie was a boisterous ten-year-old, but he was soft and gentle, too. He loved to draw things, especially the beauty of the natural world, and he was forever imagining great stories and games. He couldn't always choose the right words to say and had special difficulties with prepositions, but that didn't matter to me, as I could understand what he meant.

Unfortunately, his teachers didn't. He was held back in class and sent home with reams of spellings to get right. The headmaster wrote to mother and told her Artie would never pass his eleven plus. She was summoned to a meeting but could not bring herself to attend.

Instead, after many letters and phone calls, Mother was forced to send Artie to a secondary modern school in the next town. This meant Artie had to walk a good distance to get there, and Mother would worry every morning as he left.

"Don't talk to strangers, and go straight to school," she would cry from the front door. She never went outside, not even to walk him to school, preferring the sanctity of her home where nobody could ask questions about Isaac or pry into her life.

Sadly, Mrs. Joy was not physically able to accompany Artie either, but she still popped in at school journey time and gave him a sweet or treat to send him on his way. This ensured he wouldn't be distracted with the sweet shop en route.

Meanwhile, I continued at the local grammar school. I got on with my work, immersed myself in my studies, and tried not to think about anything else. I had few friends and so there were few questions about my family. I was very good at football and was well suited to the "beautiful game." The school needed me on the team if they were to stand any chance of ever winning a match! Football became my escape from thinking, and playing football gave me respite from always feeling responsible. Every time I laced on my tattered old boots with the missing studs, I felt a kind of release. For a few minutes, I would be free, free to run, kick, tackle, and perhaps score a goal. And whenever those goals came there was elation, perhaps magnified more than it should have been. I saw it as a small success to be savored, in my otherwise ordered and mundane life.

People rarely came to the house, but Artie kept asking Mother if he could bring some friends for tea. He was a popular boy and, frequently, would be invited over to play with his classmates. He felt embarrassed that this was never reciprocated so finally, one day, Mother gave in and Artie brought two rather scruffy schoolboys called Fred and Dennis back to our modest home.

It all went quite well. The boys were polite and ate their sandwiches, and Artie laughed and joked with them. The conversation was simple; school, football, the latest comic book heroes.

"Would you like some more sponge cake Fred?"

"Yes, please, Missus, it ain't half good!"

Soon, it was time for the boys to leave, and Fred's mother arrived to pick them up, accompanied by Fred's elder brother, Nicholas.

Nicholas was a spotty youth and clearly had been dragged along under sufferance.

Mother opened the door in response to the loud rapping, and Isaac waddled over to greet them.

"Ugh, what's that? It's a handicapped boy," sneered Nicholas "He's a Mongol; he's simple."

Fred's mother looked rather sheepish.

"Now come along boys, we must be going"

Nicholas pulled his jumper over his head and then down again.

"That's what they do. They're handicapped, ugh! Keep him away from me!" he sneered.

Mother scooped Isaac up and retreated into the kitchen

Fred's mother quickly rounded up the boys and pulled Nicholas' sleeve,

"Shush, let's go."

"But you know you don't like them! What about that weird one that lives on Sedgemore Street?"

"Shush now!"

And without another word, they were gone.

I was seething, fists balled at my side and red faced.

"And don't come back!" I yelled from the open door

Fred's mother turned around, and I could see from whom Nicholas had inherited that sneer.

I rushed back indoors and looked about for Mother.

She was sitting playing quietly with Isaac, but she couldn't hide the large tears that were rolling down her cheeks.

"It's all right, Mother. They're just idiots," I said.

She simply nodded.

2
Gee-O, 1920-1956

I was born two years after the end of the Great War; I have been told it was a time of hope and hardship. I was an afterthought, my eldest sister being nearly 20 years older than me. I was told there had also been a brother, two years younger than her. I never met him.

My father was an artist. He was frequently called upon to paint portraits of the rich and famous, hoping one day he would become so himself.

It did not happen.

When commissions were plentiful, we lived in a nice house on the outskirts of London. My father would travel by tram to his club on the river and entertain the people who wanted him to paint them.

My mother was not around much and, I think, had little interest in me, her "unwanted afterthought," I heard the servants say. My sister, Amelia, was a severe woman with a strong sense of God and duty. I understand she was responsible for looking after me in my very early years, although I never felt a particular bond with her and supposed that everything she did was out of that sense of duty.

Later, I learned that she had been let down badly by an older American soldier in the Great War. Servants told stories, and it was said that he had a wife and family waiting for him back in Kansas. They said that when Amelia learned of this, her world collapsed in an instant, and what softness and love she had squandered on her Yankee beau never returned for anyone else.

I was told that my mother was partially deaf and did not always catch what was being said to her. I attributed her distance and aloofness to this disability, but thinking back now, it was probably a ploy or device to ignore what she didn't want to hear. Arthur, my late brother, also was alleged to have poor hearing, inherited from my mother. I spent more time with the servants than anyone else when I was small, and although they didn't think I understood, I cottoned onto their gossip about my parents. I was never sure what was fact and what was fiction as they bantered and laughed at the "master's" expense. I had to decide what to believe, and that was sometimes very difficult, as the members of my family hardly ever spoke to me, so there was no help there.

In spite of his apparent handicap, I was told my brother went to a grammar school and did reasonably well. He then went to a school in preparation for the army, clearly bluffing his way through the medical if that was the case, and, in his teenage years, was sent to train as an officer cadet.

At that time, all the money my father made went into Arthur's schooling, and many years later, when there was enough, I went to school too. My own schooling was extremely hit and miss. When no one asked my father to paint their portraits, there was no money and so, there was no school for me, the last in the pecking order. I picked up enough at the odd lessons I did attend to enable me to read and write poorly. I was good at simple mathematics, but at the age of 14, when my father's life took a downward turn, there would be no more school for me ever again.

There was no doubt that, like so many other unfortunates, the Great War had scarred our family. I was told that Arthur had gone off aged 15 and fought in the trenches in France and, as such, he became a folk hero to me, the elder brother who was lost in the war, fighting for king and country. Later, I discovered, he had gone alone. Our father remained in London. Arthur disappeared during 1918. After news had reached the family of a dreadful wound, he was said to have been evacuated to a field hospital. At the end of 1918, the War office sent word to my parents that he was the missing, presumed dead.

Presumed, what an impossible word! I determined never to presume anything.

We never learned what had truly happened to poor Arthur, and so, in the end, my parents did have to presume he was dead, lost to the grasping jaws of war like so many other young men of the time.

I often wondered why my father had not gone off to be a soldier and why he had let Arthur go, a mere teenager at the time. On one occasion some years later, I remember a letter arriving for Father brought by a special postal worker. Inside it, there was a white feather. The servants told me my father had been a conscientious objector but sniggered behind their hands, and more than once, I heard them call him a coward.

My father stayed in his studio in London, hoping for more work and trying to be part of the London art scene, in spite of this stigma. As time passed, it was clear that the perceived stain on his character would not go away. He slowly withered away between the galleries and gutters in a state of penniless depression. He drank heavily. I had seen the whisky and brandy bottles lined up on his desk and sometimes watched him snoring heavily in his chair, empty bottles at his side.

My mother, supported by two spinster aunts, had a rather vague existence in a mansion in Sussex, a big old house that was apparently left to her by her father, my grandfather. I never met him. As for my father, I understood that my mother never forgave him for letting Arthur go to war alone. I do not really have any memories of my mother and father being together at all. The most family contact I had was with my elder sister Amelia, who had been put in charge of me as a baby, due, supposedly, to my mother's delicate health. It appeared that Amelia was there to chastise and berate me. I never seemed to do anything right, especially as I grew older. And so I took to disappearing, sometimes for days on end.

In my early teens, I would sneak down to the local workingmen's club, and there, one of the lads would often buy me a beer and a newspaper-wrapped portion of chips. I'd sleep rough under the stars and only slink back home again when I needed feeding properly. It was at this time in my life that I decided to run away to sea. This had been a boyhood fantasy, a dream I had when left alone. I had passed days just watching the boats come into the docks and picturing myself out on the high seas, winds howling and waves crashing; to be free as the gulls that squawked and followed the huge vessels, so majestic and unaware of the drudgery of my family life…

I didn't get very far and ended up working on the docks as an errand boy. I often slept outside and had little to eat, but somehow, I got work and kept myself alive. I wrote to my mother in Sussex, but she had no address to write back to, and she didn't send anyone to look for me. I presumed my father was drunk and uninterested in my whereabouts or my predicament, not that he knew what that was likely to be. Amelia had probably had enough. We had terrible rows, and I was rude and insolent; she, stubborn and sanctimonious. It was best we parted, and I'm sure she was relieved that I had gone.

I was forgotten.

*

After some months of this hand to mouth existence, a kindly man called Robert ("Bert" for short) took me under his wing. He was a "salt of the earth" east ender with six children and a fat and jolly wife. I met him on the docks where he did a bit of trading. He had a lung condition with great bouts of wheezing and shortness of breath. This had stopped him from being a soldier in the war, which he said was a great source of sadness for him. He was generous to a fault whenever I was concerned and wanted to take me in as his own.

"What's another mouth going to matter?" Bert wheezed jovially to his wife when he brought me to his house for the first time. "This 'ere's George – we call him Gee-O, and he'll be staying for 'is tea."

I stayed for 4 years.

Then came war: I was now 19, a gangly youth just starting to become a man and itching to prove myself in some form or another. Bert did not want me to leave but recognized that as a young man, I wanted to fight for my country. He gave me his blessing, so I joined the army.

After some basic training and a brief foray into France at the beginning of the Second World War, I was sent to train for desert warfare in Africa and the tank corps. I was in the army for six years, and I have only just started to be able to talk about it. We started out as immature and silly young men, wet behind the ears and full of bravado and pride. That didn't last long, as the reality quietly inveigled its way into our childish lives and became imprinted on our minds and souls forever. Death and destruction; loss and perpetual wounds.

No, we will never forget.

It was a strange existence. The camaraderie of the soldiers was wonderful. We were thrown together from all walks of life, plumbers and insurance clerks, dustbin men and solicitors, now together, and dependent on one another for survival.

Our basic training took place in a camp out in the Welsh countryside. Amongst the rather startled sheep and tufts of coarse grass, we wriggled in our combat gear and attacked sacks stuffed with hay with our bayonets. In the evenings, we would eat tasteless rations, potatoes and bully beef, and shine our boots to within an inch of their lives. We didn't believe that we would see proper action, and it was all rather a "Boys Own" game at that stage. A toffee-nosed captain, who had been a civil servant in civilian life, was in charge of with us and told us about our postings. He informed us that we'd be going to France and that he would be the officer in charge while we were there.

The war was not going well, and he kept trying to bolster his own importance by saying that we would sort "Gerry" out. He was such a pompous old windbag that the lads used to laugh and joke about him behind his back. After some time and lots of marching through fields and forests to his barked orders, we were whisked away from the Liverpool docks on a battered old boat and sailed up around the Scottish coast to meet up with another company in the highlands for more training and haggis bashing. All the men were terribly seasick, but somehow, it didn't affect me. I had, of course, always wanted to run away to sea, and now, here I was, all alone on deck while my mates heaved their guts out down below. I felt the irony of it, but also a sense of achievement. "Cast Iron Gee-O," they called me. We were still light years away from the reality of armed combat and the ghastliness of war, but for the first time, I felt as though I was achieving something in my own right. I got on well with the lads, and we sang and joked along together in our preparation for war.

All this jollity was short lived. Once we arrived in the muddy God-forsaken fields of France, it was a different story. There seemed to be confusion everywhere, and before long, our great captain was pulling us back from the front line, fussing and twitching about the German advance. We lost many good soldiers. Screaming and dying men littered the northern shores of France, and the deafening sound of gunfire and cannon invaded our every waking moment. My little company stayed together and was lucky enough to be first back onto the beaches. We clambered into anything that floated and soon were scattered across the British channel in an array of little boats, some hardly seaworthy, trying to get home from Dunkirk. The men's spirits were dowsed. Brash seawater pounded our gallant vessels as we sailed nervously back across the channel in dreadful retreat. The company was defeated, and we tucked our tails between our legs, patched up the wounded, and went back to camp in Wales to recover.

I was badly shaken, like all the other lads, and we smoked and smoked to calm our shattered nerves. Back in Wales, the mood was somber, and we were grateful for the rigorous discipline of army life to distract us from thinking too much about what had happened and particularly about our fallen comrades.

Finally, after "Mr. Pomposity" had been replaced by a much more down to earth captain, it was time to see action again. This time, we were to be sent to North Africa and the tank corps.

After it was over, those years of bloodshed and conflict, a lot of the war became a blur to me.

There was, however, one particular bloody encounter with a German patrol that I remembered forever. Our lads won the day all right; and I should have been happy for that, but at the time, I was terrified it was my bullets that had been responsible for the death of others. I couldn't come to terms with the awful possibility that I might have, probably had, taken human life! War made murderers of us all, and that broke something inside me.

There had been six of us in the squad, which had been led by a burly well-muscled sergeant. We'd come together after basic training and had traded cigarettes and bawdy stories to keep our spirits up during the time so far in North Africa. That particular night, we were patrolling a small village just as dusk was settling. The sights and sounds of that war-torn desert hole were amplified by the expectancy of attack.

"Over there," my sergeant hissed. I could just make out some robed bodies in a blown-out, mud house. One suddenly stood up and yelled.

In an instant, there was gunfire all around us. We dived for cover behind some jagged rocks and fired back. Four German soldiers ran towards the house firing indiscriminately, presumably, thinking we were in there. They had their backs to us. Someone yelled an order to fire, but it wasn't clear where it had come from. All at once, each of us fired into the melee, and for a few seconds there was smoke and screams and bedlam. I must have fired off all the rounds I had, but my eyes were squeezed tightly shut. When the dust settled and the firecracker noise of gunfire ceased, there were four blood-soaked German soldiers face down on the ground; none could have been more than 18 years old. With them lay an old kefir, sprawled without dignity in a pool of his own blood. I stood still, frozen to the spot. The sergeant and others gingerly approached the scene of carnage and prodded the bodies.

"Best leave 'em," the sergeant said, "bound to be more around…"

We slunk back into the shadows where we had come from, under the ever-darkening skies. I remember my feet moving as though I were an automaton. Had I been responsible for those deaths? Shot in the back… Cowardly! Had it been my bullets that hit them? I would never know, but I desperately hoped not to have been responsible. It was then that I understood why my father had not wanted to partake in this senseless, stupid activity called war. What on earth were we doing?

"Them or us," "them or us," the mantra sung out over and over. "Kill the swine," "Take 'em out," "Get the buggers!" But they were just young men like us.

Back at camp, I started to get strange symptoms: sweaty palms, palpitations, and a feeling of not belonging. I couldn't make the feelings go away. Sometimes, they would go, only to come back with such ferocity that I could hardly move or speak. My whole body was in a constant state of tension, my mind stunned into blankness.

Perhaps it was the war and my way of blocking out the horrors, but after that incident, my mind would make me feel like I belonged in another universe. Perhaps I was in another universe…? I *wanted* to be in another universe, one without pain or bloodshed, or guilt and shame.

*

"Private Galley," said a nurse's voice from above me. "You're in the military hospital in Tobruk. Can you hear me?"

I slowly took in my surroundings. A whitewashed room, hot and stuffy, and all around me, the muffled groans of men in pain and anguish. Some were physical, some mental. A breeze fluttered through open windows, and row upon row of cast iron beds lined the ward, which was bathed in a fine layer of dust and sand. A nurse in a starched uniform rushed around with bedpans. The heat was stifling and my head was pounding.

I couldn't remember anything; my body felt as though it didn't belong to me, and those wretched symptoms started again. I leaned over the side of the bed and heaved my entire innards into a china bowl.

"It's all right soldier. You're safe here."

The nurse tried to sound reassuring, but I felt detached and alone. Nothing could stop the swirling dust, which seemed to insinuate itself into everything, everywhere. It was in my brain, clogging up my thoughts. My mind was a blur, and I had the feeling that time was merging into itself. I must have been in the hospital for several weeks, in a kind of limbo existence between reality and fantasy. During that time, I received letters. They piled up by the side of my bed, but I was too distracted by my symptoms to read any of them properly.

When I did finally emerge from my stupor I realised that Sally, Bert's eldest daughter, must have taken a bit of a shine to me. She was a pretty little thing, and four years older than me. War had intervened before anything had happened between us, but I had inkling at the time that she might have been soft on me.

She wrote every day; long chatty letters in her large loopy handwriting. I tried to concentrate on the words, but they fell away into a deep dark hole, a deep trough with nothing left in it – that chasm that was my mind.

My memory slowly returned, and the scar on my head healed. They told me I'd been shot and the bullet had grazed my skull, but I did not think that was the real cause of my war wound. My mind had broken.

Again, I tried to read Sally's letters, but the words jumbled together, and I couldn't concentrate. I felt bad; because Sally continued not to feature in my broken thoughts and her letters, piled at my bedside, were a reminder of the frustration I felt, the inability to get back to normal, to before the war and all its horrors.

Nurses wheeled wounded soldiers outside for air, day after day; gave us bed baths, dressed the visible wounds, and served us simple food in an attempt to mend us. Every so often, a new batch of broken men would arrive, and the nurses would rush round in a frenzy, trying to deal with the onslaught. Then, the ward would slowly calm, and one by one, the inmates would either recover or succumb.

Miraculously, I was one of the ones who got better and was, I thought, back to normal when I returned to England, invalided out of the war. There was much celebration at Bert's house after our ship docked in London. Sally and Bert had been there to meet me and whisked me off to the pub. They sat and smiled as I downed my first English pint for months. They seemed so pleased to have me home, but I felt numb inside. The beer did nothing for me.

The war dragged on another year, through some of the bleakest moments in history. There were bombings, and so much heartache as families were split asunder. I lived through all of this in a fog. Sally seemed to be at my side, smiling and cajoling. Food appeared on my plate at mealtimes, and I must have eaten it. I don't remember doing anything except walking. Miles upon miles, I walked to escape, escape from my inner thoughts. I couldn't connect to the world, and although I was given newspapers to read, I can't remember taking in a single word. This dreamlike existence seemed useless and pointless, but still, it went on. All around me were tales of another son lost, another husband gone missing. Yet here I was, back at home, cozy and warm and well-fed and… guilty; guilty of abandoning my post, of abandoning my mind.

Finally, and for no obvious reason, my torture came to an end. The mist lifted, the gloom dissipated, and I could see the sun again; time, the universal healer. I could hear the springtime choruses of courting songbirds, could see the sky and moon and stars at night. Somehow, reality had crept back and pushed away the madness, and I felt what it was to be human once more.

Sally and I started walking out.

There wasn't much work in the area, but Bert got me a job in a nearby factory. It was a large, noisy building with red brick walls in a state of disrepair but still standing in spite of the bombardments during the blitz. I put on workman's overalls and took on a workman's swagger and started to make my way up the pecking order of life.

Things were tough, but I told myself that Sally and I could be happy together, walking along the docks in the moonlight. Sally would dream. She would dream of a little house, lots of kids, and a nice little garden. It was clear what she wanted. I drifted along with it, but I had never been sure what my own future should be. My boyhood dreams had been of the sea and glory. None of this had come to pass. I did my best to bury what few memories I had of the war and lived from day today.

Deep down, I think I still longed for the freedom of the sea; at least, I imagined that was what I longed for. Maybe I just wanted freedom, freedom from my life, from my inner demons, from my fear. I didn't want to have to think or take responsibility, so I allowed Sally to make decisions for both of us and hoped for the best. I went along with it, all in a kind of hazy resignation.

Bert started to make hints. I knew that he wanted me to propose to Sally, but still, I was reluctant.

It was what he wanted, but did I want that too? Perhaps it didn't matter what I wanted, and it was time now for me to do my duty, do the right thing.

*

I had lost my virginity while in the army, a fumble and tumble in a local house of disrepute in London before I was posted to Wales. Sometimes I would travel back to that forbidden place, on the quiet. There had been a beautiful girl who worked in the brothel, but I couldn't afford her. I would go to the house just to see if I could steal a glimpse of her. When at last I did see her through one of the windows, it was as if the whole world had been illuminated, the colours and sounds so clear and beautiful. I never even went in again. I think the Madame in charge thought I was soft in the head when she saw me pacing up and down outside.

One day, purely by chance, I saw the lovely girl in the street, not far from the 'workplace'.

I tripped my way across the road to her and blurted out some rubbish.

"Hey pretty boy," she said mockingly. "Haven't I seen you before?"

"I love you," I murmured, not even sure if she had heard me. She walked on by chatting and giggling to her friend. I bowed my head, trembling.

I shrank into the shadows of the buildings around me and scurried off, like some unwanted rodent that had been caught stealing food, embarrassed and broken hearted. I took the train home, cursing the world as I sat gazing through the murky carriage window and arrived back, late for tea.

Sally greeted me, having no idea that my heart had been engaged elsewhere. If that was love, you could keep it. Keep the pain and humiliation. I never went back to the brothel, and I buried thoughts of love deep inside my tortured mind. I had to move on. Could I ever learn to love Sally like that?

Finally, I plucked up the courage to speak to Bert. I knew Sally was a good girl and loved me unconditionally, heaven only knew why. Bert was delighted and gave me an old ring that had been his grandmother's.

"We should keep it in the family," he said

That evening, feeling rather self-conscious, with the docks in the background and the East End of London looking on, I went down on one knee and asked Sally to marry me.

*

We had a small and simple ceremony in an old church with crumbling walls, a tiny interior that served to witness the marriage, and a priest more than happy to oblige. Sally chose the church hall for the small party afterwards. It seemed fitting that our marriage should take place somewhere that was held together with prayers and string. The big day loomed, and even at the eleventh hour, I had fleeting thoughts of escaping to the coast.

My mother and aunts were invited, but they did not attend. Amelia arrived in a somber dress more fitting for a funeral than a wedding. Bert was generous as ever in his speech and in paying for the celebration afterwards. I daresay he had a few too many beers, but Sally beamed at him when a tear left his eye as he said Sally was the best daughter a father could ever wish for. Sally looked sweet in her white gown. Her small frame and kindly features were made to look so special. She had a very petite face with soft grey eyes that smiled unsolicited at everyone. Her brown, rather mousy hair was piled high on her head and kept in place by a small veil that made her look even more childlike.

Did I love her?

By then I had decided that, whatever love was, this was good enough for me, and I determined to enjoy the day that these kind people had put so much effort into. A pang of guilt passed quickly when Bert slapped me on the back and said he expected a large brood of lusty lunged Galleys. I was beginning to settle into the pathway my life had taken and joined in with a rousing chorus of "Danny Boy" late into the evening.

Married life was pleasant and ordered and Sally was attentive to my every need. She would do anything for me, asked or silently requested, and she would never hear a word against me or answer back if I raised my voice. Work was hard, and I was too exhausted to think about much else. The awful war memories faded, and my low self-esteem was firmly placed on the back burner to slowly simmer unguarded.

After a year or so, the factory started running into difficulty. I talked with Bert, and we agreed I needed to find a job in a less expensive area. Eventually, I found something further north, but it meant uprooting everything. Bert was sad to see us go, but he couldn't help any more. He was getting old and unsteady in himself.

We found a little terraced house that we could afford to buy, and I started my job in the nearby works as an apprentice engineer.

My first son was born in 1948, and we named him George, after me. He would be called George, I determined, and not Gee-O, which I had never liked.

I still didn't really understand where the nickname had come from. My father never called me anything but "boy," and my mother hardly spoke at all. An old housekeeper had called me Gee-O or possibly Gee-up as I cavorted round the kitchen on my poor dead brother's hobbyhorse. The hobbyhorse was taken away, but Gee-O seemed to stick, more's the pity. Bert embraced my nickname wholeheartedly and treated me like a long-lost son. I hadn't the heart to upset him. So, when I finally married, it gave me a strange feeling to be called Gee-O by my father-in-law.

Now, I was a father; I vowed my son would have no nickname.

I felt proud but empty. Sally devoted her attention to George, who was rather a solemn little chap and I drifted along on my own path. I was doing quite well at the factory and could send back a small sum of money to Bert, who was now completely incapacitated. Sally was over the moon with our little family and our house, even though everything in it was secondhand and drab.

I found myself travelling around the country as part of the sales project for the factory. I didn't miss being at home. It all just unfolded as it would, and I sailed along on the tide of it without too much emotional input.

My favorite place was Brighton, where I became great friends with a couple named Gareth and Cynthia, who ran a small hotel on the outskirts of the bustling town. The sea air was so refreshing, and I loved to walk along the shingle and gaze out to the horizon. The crashing waves seemed to say they could wash away the uncertainty that surrounded me, each one giving a promise of a new start. I suppose I still hankered after going to sea as I did as a 14-year-old, unsure of what it really meant. Was the grass always greener? Or in this case, the waves?

Our lives progressed, and for all intents and purposes, we were happy.

A second son was born a few years later, and we continued to live in our little terraced house.

In 1956, when Arthur was four, Sally kept on at me about having another child. I was as content as I could be and didn't want to upset anything, but she had come from a big family and wanted more children. She was nearly 40 now, and I didn't think it was wise.

One day she announced she was pregnant.

"But you said you were using that device?"

"Perhaps it didn't work or something. Anyway, isn't it great news?"

I felt cornered and, not for the first time, started to get odd sickening feelings in the pit of my stomach.

Of course, Bert was over the moon and on about us having a "football team."

Sally's pregnancy was different. She was much smaller, and when she went into labour four weeks before her allotted time, I knew things weren't right. The boy was born at home, and I saw at once that he was different. I had heard about Down syndrome.

Not many people knew of it, but for some reason, maybe fate, I had read about it in a medical textbook. I was reading about anxiety. I had got the book from the library to try and make some sense of my own condition. I wanted to know if my condition had been inherited, and I found myself looking at diseases and conditions that were genetically determined. A short paragraph on

Down syndrome had stuck in my memory. I had struggled with the difficult words in the book and had asked the librarian to read it out to me. The mongoloid features, the mental handicap, the slowness and physical problems; I didn't think then that it could happen to my family.

The doctor was very brusque and business like and asked us if we wanted the baby to be taken away to a home. I thought it best, but Sally would have none of it. So, he stayed.

And I had to leave.

It wasn't that I didn't love him; I did in my own way. But when I saw him, my symptoms started, and I felt the whole world closing in. I simply couldn't cope.

I went to Brighton.

When I arrived, Cynthia could see I was troubled. She called Gareth, and together, they sat me down. They had been wonderful to me, and I think they rather thought of me as their little misfit. I was a loner, a stranger in need of solace, and they wanted a project, a mission now that their own children had left home. They ran a sweet hotel with a dozen rooms and a lovely dining room with a sea view. I would linger over breakfasts there, and little by little, I would talk to both Cynthia and Gareth in turn. Away from the real world, I opened up to them, and they knew I wasn't happy. When I appeared in a somewhat agitated state, they took me into their private parlour and fixed me a strong whisky.

"I've left Sally" I moaned and proceeded to tell them about baby Isaac and the terrible symptoms I was experiencing. They nodded and sighed and listened.

Those dear friends in the hotel gave me a job and paid me well. I stayed in one of the rooms overlooking the sea, and I did every little job that was needed for them, any time of the day or night. In return, I was well fed and was able to send a little money back to Sally. Night after night, I would listen to the crashing waves, agonizing about what I should do. My symptoms would then start up again, and I'd be rooted to the bed in a pool of cold sweat, waiting for some relief. Eventually, it would come, and I realised to stop the symptoms I had to stop thinking of Sally and Isaac.

Poor Sally.

She hated me for abandoning them all.

It became harder and harder for me to go back, so I didn't.

3
Amelia, 1900-1956

I wasn't always like this. I am sure I had been a happy, carefree young woman, perhaps for a while, all those years ago. I had come to understand that life was cruel and indiscriminate. It took you and shook you when you least expected it. I was wary now; I wasn't going to let that happen ever again. I built my walls, slowly and surely, they became impenetrable.

Even now, I do not recognize who I am any more.

Can you picture a small girl, long flowing hair streaming behind her as she ran carefree down a grassy bank?

Yes, that was me all those years ago. Now, she's lost. Gone forever.

My father, an artist of some talent, would call my brother and I to his musty study, where he would make us sit incredibly still while he attempted to paint our images. I remember feeling terrified and elated at the same time. Terrified that if I moved, my father would bark at me, and elated that, in time, there would be a real picture of me. How would I look? What features would my father concentrate on? My hair, if only I didn't have so much hair. I was never really able to tame it. I wasn't vain, well, that's what I told myself, but I wanted to know what others saw, what my father saw, when he looked at me.

It was 1912, and our lives were comfortable and ordered. We lived in a nice house on the outskirts of London. We, like many so called middle class families, had a batch of servants. They were treated and paid well and did their jobs without comment or dissent. My mother was rarely seen, and our Nanny would look after us most of the time. The governess would come once a week to teach me. I was schooled in piano and art and needlepoint, thought to be essential for a young lady of my standing. My younger brother would go off with Mr. Jackson, a young Cambridge graduate, to learn about what boys should learn about. He later went to a highly respected grammar school and then joined an army academy and trained to be a soldier. I can't say I was sad to see him go. He irritated me and played pranks and behaved badly, then tried to blame me. My father and mother would always take his side – not that they were around very much.

We children were dressed neatly (apart from my hair, which would just not be controlled!) and behaved properly when in company. The cook gave us home-baked biscuits and a slice of freshly baked cake if we were good, and the parlour maid played cards with us when her chores were done and noone else was around.

Then came the war.

There were raised voices and slammed doors. Servants rushed about, the younger males going off to enlist, and the maids weeping on the steps for their sweethearts. My mother suddenly appeared after months away with her two severe sisters. She told me I was going to the country with them. War was upon us, and my father would have to join the army and fight, she said. I did not understand until later why he had never left for France. Rumors abounded, and when Arthur, aged 15, ran off to the trenches without a restraining hand from him, my father's reputation and good name came under fire. He was drinking a lot, and my mother quietly, but firmly, left him in London. For two years, I lived with my mother and her sisters down in Rye. The war raged in France, and food was short in London. We were well-looked after though and moved in quite high social circles in Sussex. My mother drew a veil over her emotions, and if she mourned Arthur and his "loss," she never showed it.

She showed no emotion toward me either. We did not feel the privations felt by others during this terrible war. We were somehow immune; my mother and aunts never spoke of much, and when asked where father was, they replied, he was busy with his clients. It was as if the family had given what they could in the way of Arthur and now wanted to be left alone.

We settled into a comfortable routine, and my mother hosted little soirees from time to time. We were forbidden to read the newspapers and to talk to anyone in the nearby village. It was as if my mother would have nothing to do with the reality of the fighting, preferring to hold onto the social structure that had preceded the dreadful onset of this Great War.

In early 1918, an American family was visiting the area. I understood that the father, a Major Steinberg, was a distant relative of the local bishop. He and his wife had five screaming children, and I did not relish the thought of meeting them and having to be polite to their ghastly offspring. My mother, not usually excitable, was very anxious to entertain the Major and his family. Our country house was fairly large with a sweeping drive through a small wood that opened out to reveal an imposing house and gardens. I never knew to whom it originally belonged but assumed it had been my grandfather's in his time. The family never spoke about this, but I had heard that my grandfather had been a successful financier. And all successful financiers were Jews. This was never mentioned or discussed in public, but I picked up little tidbits from the servants and village folk. There was clearly money in our family, and it didn't come from my father, so the wealth must have come from my grandfather. He had died somewhere in Germany before the war, and my grandmother had apparently stayed there, distraught and bereft, until she too perished.

One day, on one of the few occasions that my mother addressed me directly, I was informed that a soiree had been arranged for late summer. I was relieved to hear that this would be a grown-up affair with no children invited. My mother said that I was to be allowed to participate as long as I did not speak to anyone of my father or the war. I happily agreed and thought that at last, I might now meet some interesting people and have an opportunity to come out into the world of which I knew so very little.

On the allotted day, the sky was an azure blue, and the sun beat down on the already scorched land. There had been a heat wave for many weeks in the little southeastern corner of Britain, and the village longed for some break in the weather. The Major and other guests arrived in horse drawn carriages. I had been allowed a new frock for the occasion and was eager to join adult society properly for the first time. So, on that balmy evening in August, the carriages arrived and disgorged their elegant passengers. A dashing young officer who was dancing attendance on the Major and his rather silly wife immediately took my eye.

As the party neared the entrance, my mother and aunts received the guests, and I stood back from them, waiting to shake hands.

"Major Steinberg and Missus Steinberg, how lovely to see you," cooed my mother. I couldn't help noticing a look that passed between her and the major.

"And this is Lieutenant John Partridge, my secretary," he pronounced Lieutenant as "loo-tenant," the American way.

"Call me Jack," the lieutenant said as he squeezed my hand warmly.

The evening progressed, and my mother and aunts were circulating and chatting to each of the guests. I noticed that Missus Steinberg attracted a group of young men led by the handsome lieutenant. She sat in the middle and tittered and blushed, waving her fan furiously, pretending to swoon with the heat. My mother, meanwhile, had monopolized the major and was tucked in a darkened corner of the ballroom with him.

I sat down on a little stool some way from the main party and stared at all the women in their gowns and the men in their evening suits and uniforms. It was not a huge party, maybe 25 or so, but it felt overpoweringly stifling. I suddenly was aware of a figure standing by me.

"You ladies look so pretty," Jack drawled in a deep Southern American accent. "I feel so blessed to be here and meeting y'all this evening. But come, now, why aren't you chatting away? You can't be shy, now can you?"

He was laughing at me, and I felt tongue tied and juvenile.

"I'm just catching some air," I said in as grown up a voice as I could muster.

"Well, Missy Amelia…" He had remembered my name, and my heart nearly stopped. "Would you do me the honour of showing me these pretty little gardens? I'm sure they'll be plenty of air out there."

The stiflingly hot breeze and sounds of grasshoppers in the field was overpowering as I found myself walking side-by-side with this handsome soldier.

"What do you do?" I asked rather crassly.

"Oh, I look after Major Steinberg and his wife. He's a good sort; she's a fluffy little thing, just good at reproducing. I believe the major is here to talk about the war with some bigwigs in London, but he made a special point of wanting to see your mother."

I was stunned at the lack of candour in his conversation.

"How does he know her?"

"Oh, I believe they met in New York."

"New York? I didn't know my mother had been there."

"Oh, yes," said Jack. "She comes over quite a lot."

I was stunned. Her absences from the family home had never been explained, but here was this easy American telling me all the family secrets at our first meeting. We came upon a small bench under a weeping willow tree, out of sight of the guests

"Shall we sit here a while?"

Jack talked and talked about America, and the cotton plantations, and the Negroes who worked them, and life in the army. I hung on his every word. He told of Missus Steinberg and her flirtations and being pregnant every other minute, and of the major and his money.

I realised that I was staring hopelessly at this charismatic man. I had never had any acquaintances that were male and only a couple of girlfriends in Sussex. I was awkward and felt self-conscious, lacking in social skills.

"You're a pretty little thing, you know that?" grinned Jack. "I've a mind to ask you out for tea tomorrow. The major is having a quiet day and says I can have the afternoon free, what do you say?"

I must have nodded like a lunatic.

We walked slowly back to the party, but no one took much notice of us. I did see Cook, though, and she had a troubled countenance. This passed me by with little comprehension at the time.

For the rest of the evening, Jack did his duty and was gregarious and charming. I simply couldn't take my eyes off him and ran to the gate as his carriage left late in the evening. He did not wave, but I could feel his eyes on me as the carriage bearing him and the major and his wife swept out of the grounds.

I couldn't sleep. The night was heavy and humid, but my thoughts were full of Jack and his flashing eyes. I was smitten.

The next afternoon couldn't come fast enough. Jack had spoken to my mother, who had agreed that I could take tea in Rye with him. She decided it would be good for me to get out a bit. She would take me herself in our carriage, as she wanted to pay a visit to the Major to do some business. I didn't question the arrangement and was duly deposited at Aunt Betty's tearooms, where gallant Jack was on hand to meet me. Once again, the sky was an impossible blue, and the sun lit up the world in a glorious heat haze. I heard birdsong for the first time in my life, although, of course, I must have heard it often enough before but never registered it with such clarity. It was as though my senses were on high alert.

We took tea and chatted and chatted all afternoon. Jack made me laugh with his impersonations of the major and also my aunts.

"I hope I'm not being too forward!" he drawled, but it was obvious to anyone around that he didn't care.

I never did notice my mother and the major walking arm and arm down the street to a small house at the end of the village. I was so engrossed in Jack that I also didn't notice the time passing, and soon, it was six o'clock.

"Oh, my goodness! My mother should have been here ages ago to collect me. What do you think could have happened?"

"Don't trouble your pretty little head. I'll escort you home, that's if you don't mind walking a-ways?"

I was glad to and, as there was no sign of my mother or aunts to get me, thought that the best option.

We walked out through the tree lined street and up over the fields. Jack had taken off his jacket in the heat and threw it over his shoulder. I could see the muscles rippling through his damp white shirt, and I must have caught my breath. I turned away quickly, but I could hear Jack laughing at me. We came to a little copse, and suddenly, Jack had whisked me up in his arms and was kissing me passionately. I didn't know how to react, and although I gave a little struggle, I was completely melting into him. He pressed me down on the ground and began to run his hands all over my body.

"No! What... Oh goodness!" I gasped between kisses.

Before I knew it, he was entering me, and a searing pain ripped through my loins.

"Oh God!" I cried, but he held me tighter and tighter. I succumbed to his passion, and my mind was in turmoil. I moved rhythmically to his thrusting, not understanding what was happening. And then it was all over.

I looked down at my tattered dress

"Don't you worry," Jack grinned. "We can say we got caught up in these here brambles."

He brushed himself down and grabbed my arm, somewhat roughly. "You'll be mine, always, won't you?" He grinned again.

"And best not to tell, we don't want anyone spoiling this, do we?"

I nodded and tried to get my breath. My legs felt weak, and my heart was racing. He pulled me up, and I was propelled along on his strong arm. We must have walked for a mile or so, but my feet didn't seem to touch the ground, and soon, we were back at the house.

"My, what's happened to you!" gasped Cook when she saw me.

"Had a tangle with some brambles on the way home," said Jack, in a very matter-of-fact voice.

Cook was fussing over me, and I was helpless as Jack moved to the door.

"It's been a pleasure, Missy Amelia," he said.

And with that, he was gone.

*

My mother did not appear to notice what had happened to me, but I knew Cook did, and I'm sure she saw the bloodstain on my underskirt.

The next day, sore and bruised, I waited for Jack to call. Mother said she was off to town to do more business with the major.

Jack never returned.

I finally plucked up courage to ask mother one evening about the Americans.

"Mother, has Lieutenant Partridge asked after me again? I thought he might want to have tea sometime." I tried to sound disinterested.

"No, dear. The major and his aide have gone up to London. I'm not sure we'll see them again this trip."

My heart sank, my body and mind in confusion. I was besotted with Jack and had thought he wanted me for all time.

"Anyway, I believe Lieutenant Partridge will be leaving England soon. I understand his wife is expecting another baby."

Her words cut like a knife. I don't know if she realised what she was doing to me or not. Sometimes, looking back on that moment, I believed she knew everything. But at the time, my mother didn't appear to notice my ashen face, or how I reeled out of the room, only just making it to the bathroom before I heaved and heaved. My world disintegrated in that instant, never to recover.

A few weeks passed, and my mood plummeted. I cried softly into my pillow at night and couldn't eat. Only Cook noticed and kept trying to tempt me with morsels that she knew I usually loved. My mother was oblivious and much taken up with her own "business." I even missed poor Arthur and our spats. He and I never got on, and I think he was always jealous that he had not been first born.

That would have endowed even more power on him than Victorian England already allowed. But he was gone, probably dead in some trench, oh, how awful! I couldn't bear to think of it.

After two months, I started feeling bloated and sick. I did not comprehend what this meant. The parlour maid found me crying one morning in the conservatory and took me back into my bedroom. She asked me if I'd seen my monthlies, as she didn't recall washing out any rags that month.

"What is it?" I cried.

"Oh Lord," she said. "I think you might be pregnant."

"No, no!" I sobbed, and she held me tightly

"We'll have to tell the missus."

"No, please no!" I was almost hysterical, and it was all she could do to calm me down.

"We'll wait a couple of days and see if it comes."

A week later, I had avoided all contact and was sneaking around the house from room to room, trying to be invisible. The maid found me and took me back to my room once more.

I lay on the bed and sobbed and sobbed

"Look, you can't hide forever," she soothed

Then suddenly, I got a cramping pain down in my abdomen.

"It's coming!" I exclaimed

"Thank God," said the maid. "I'll get you some hot tea."

For hours, the pains surged around my body. This wasn't like anything I'd experienced before. And there was no blood.

I felt weaker and weaker, and then, two days later, I started pouring. It came and came and wouldn't stop. The maid was terrified and fled to get the doctor. I heard her encounter with my mother as she left.

"Miss Amelia is very poorly, and I'm going for the doctor!"

"Surely it's just a stomach cramp." My mother sighed. "Well, you best get him if you want, but it's probably just Amelia being hysterical, as usual."

"I don't think so Ma'am," but I could tell my mother was long since gone.

The doctor came and gave me some sort of sleeping draught. I could still hear the conversation even though they thought I was asleep, as the maid asked the doctor what he thought was wrong.

"I suspect from what you've told me that she is having a miscarriage, and I don't anticipate she will ever be likely to conceive again. Does her mother know?"

"Oh, no sir, please, couldn't we just look after her here, and not bother the missus?"

The doctor grunted and left, and I never knew whether he spoke to my mother or not.

Slowly, the bleeding stopped and I grew a little stronger. Cook and the maid brought me broth and fruit and tidbits and watched and waited. My mother did not appear. The maid told me that my mother had sent her regards, hoped I was feeling better, but had urgent business in London.

Weeks passed, and eventually I got out of bed and started to eat a little more. Months passed, and I dragged myself outside and took gentle walks. I spoke very little, felt wretched, and considered myself a complete failure. I convinced myself that Jack had discarded me because I was evil. Evil because I had perhaps enjoyed what he had done to me, brought it on myself, led him on. I must have known he was married, mustn't I? My internal anger and hatred of myself knew no bounds. I dressed in black and moped about the house like a lost soul. I cut off all my hair and wore a mobcap to hide the uneven mess underneath.

A letter came from my father. He said we were to leave at once for London and that my mother was in great need of me.

I was stunned and could not understand the summons.

My aunts came with me, and I arrived back in London at my father's house.

My mother was expecting again and wanted me to look after her and then care for the baby when it arrived. I could hardly string two words together, but somehow, I managed to accede. My mother's health was delicate, my father maintained.

I was like a wraith and a shadow, and I crept about doing whatever my mother bade me. One evening, I had gone to my room but just before I shut the door I heard raised voices. My mother was speaking in a harsh whisper.

"You will be a father to this baby, or else this lifestyle that you have become so accustomed to will cease"

"Why should I be a father to the little bastard?"

"Because that is how it will be. Amelia can look after the child when it is born, she needs something to do, a distraction. We will remain a family as far as society is concerned. I want nothing to do with the child myself, and you can do as you please. But I will not have a scandal, do you hear!"

Thoughts tumbled around in my head as I tried to piece everything together. At nearly 20 years old, I grew up rapidly. I realised I was just a pawn in a much bigger game. I decided there and then to do my duty and keep quiet. Perhaps one day God would forgive me for my own indiscretions.

My mother went through a difficult labour and gave birth to a lusty baby boy. As soon as the doctors would allow, my aunts whisked her off back to Sussex, and I was left in charge of the infant with a wet nurse. The nurse showed me what to do, and I cared for young George with a strict regime. I did not pick him up if he cried until it was the correct time. I changed him roughly and put him in his crib without soothing him first, unlike the wet nurse. I did not hate him, and I realised it was not his fault, but he represented everything that had gone wrong in my life. My father never came near the child, and if he was inadvertently in the same room, he left almost immediately.

I did my duty, hoping it would assuage my guilt and sorrow. I was a surrogate and spent my life with little George, inadvertently and slowly developing a tempered affection for him. In spite of myself, I couldn't always be angry with him, especially when he smiled or did something sweet. This was not very often, and I kept myself in check. I didn't deserve to be happy, no one did.

Soon George was a toddler. The cook and parlour maid loved him, and that blackened my mood even more. They called him Gee-O, a ridiculous name, but I didn't change it, as I didn't care. Gee-O it was. I insisted at least it be spelt Geo.

Eventually, we were invited back to Sussex for a brief stay. Relationships between my mother and father were at an all-time low, and it became clear that my mother was going to spend all her time in the country dwelling. We returned to London, no better off for seeing my self-absorbed mother.

Geo grew and grew and became a gangly teenager. Sometimes he went to school, but often, my father had no money, and it seemed my mother wasn't interested in helping out from her own personal funds any more.

Time passed, life passed me by. I had no friends. I was enveloped in my shroud of hate and misery, broken only by my sense of duty. I tried to get on with Geo, but he was a lonely young boy and often would run away. One day, he never came back.

I stayed in London and looked after my father for his remaining years. The money ran out, and we lived a frugal existence without servants, long since dismissed through lack of funds. My father drank more and more, and often, the police would haul him home and drop him on the doorstep.

One day my hopeless father finally succumbed to his precious brandy. I wrote and told Geo, but the letter was returned some weeks later, *not known at this address*.

I did, however, receive a letter from Geo some years afterward, telling me he was getting married. Something in me thawed, and I decided to attend. It was a jolly affair, as only East end weddings can be. I could see, even though I hadn't seen Geo for years, that he was not as besotted with his bride as he should have been. No doubt, he was damaged too. I spoke civilly to him and left a small present. He thanked me, and I was surprised to get letters from him on a fairly regular basis. I took to visiting occasionally, and it gave me the small sense of belonging that I had never really felt in my entire life. Geo asked me to help with his two small boys when his wife was indisposed from time to time, and I almost became attached to them, in spite of their unruliness.

Then, Isaac was born.

It was a disaster for them all. I tried to help with their dreadful undisciplined children while Sally was unwell, but I left as soon as I could. At the age of 56, my life had disappeared.

I never heard anything of what may have happened to Major Steinberg or Jack, and that episode in my life gradually faded. Deep down, the wounds never healed, and even now I cry myself to sleep and remember the physicality of our brief liaison.

I have two cats; they roam free and come back to take food and shelter when they choose. That is the closest I have got to another relationship. I understand the cats, and they take from me what I am prepared to give. I do not crave anything else anymore.

4
George, 1962-1968

After the incident with Nicholas, I became more protective of Isaac. Mother now had even fewer friends.

Isaac grew and attempted to say a few words, only recognizable to us. He also started to dance whenever he heard music on the radio. He loved it, and it was a great way of getting him out of a bad mood or a strop.

Grandpa Bert came when he could, but you could see he was uncomfortable near Isaac, and his emphysema was getting worse.

I decided that for my part, I had to do well with my studies at school to get on in life, to support the family as best I could. I determined to try and go to university.

My father, never seen, was sending money, and I knew that my mother had an address for him. I asked her if I could write to my father. She looked surprised but left her little address book open on the kitchen table.

I decided to ask my father for money to help me through university. I told him I didn't want to see him, but that he owed it to the family. I would then be able to get a good job and look after Isaac and mother, thus releasing father from his obligation. Father would then be able to stop sending money and need not contact us again. I pondered over the wording for hours but eventually was satisfied. It was a letter devoid of feeling, signed, "George, your son."

Around that time, Isaac's behavior started to deteriorate. At the age of eight, he had put on weight, and as he loved his food, which was difficult to deny him, this trend accelerated. Most of the time, he was a happy little chap, but as he reached puberty, he became unpredictable. The nights were the worst, and Artie and I had to take it in turns to hold him. Occasionally, he would lash out, presumably in frustration, and my poor mother did not know what to do. We tried to help as best we could, sometimes taking hours just to get him into bed or brush his teeth, which by now were sadly beginning to decay. By the age of 10, Isaac was losing his happy-go-lucky little self and was too strong for my mother to handle.

I was desperate to do well in my exams. I had no time for anything else, and Artie was struggling at school. I read up as much as I could on Down syndrome and realised that it was likely he was hypothyroid, a condition where one of his glands wasn't producing enough energy hormone. Obesity was a possible outcome of the condition. There wasn't much on mood swings though, and Isaac seemed to display these a lot.

My mother could see it was hopeless and called the doctor for some help and advice. Before we knew it, the doctor had arranged for Isaac to be admitted to a hospital to be looked after. One day, they took him away.

My mother went by bus to see him every day, and Artie and I would go at weekends when we could.

The hospital was like an old gothic castle with huge grounds full of beautiful rhododendrons that did little to blunt the austerity of the surroundings. The ward Isaac was admitted to was vast and full of poor creatures with all sorts of neurological and mental diseases. Isaac was next to a skinny boy who just lay on his bed all day. The nurse told us that the boy had epilepsy and required lots of medication to stop him fitting.

They gave Isaac medication too. He was subdued. He didn't communicate much, and the few words that he could say had disappeared. We sat by him, sometimes trying to read his favorite book to him or cajole him to eat, but he pulled away and rocked back and forth, turning his head to the wall. We were so distressed to see him like that.

"But at least he's safe here, Mum," I said, unconvincingly.

Mother looked away.

One day, when we went to visit Isaac, we couldn't see him in his usual spot.

"Perhaps he's in the toilet," one of the nurses said as she whisked by.

As he didn't come out for some time, I told mother I would go and look for him.

I found him lying on the toilet floor, foaming at the mouth with his eyes rolled back. I yelled for a nurse and two burly men arrived to pick him up. It wasn't an epileptic fit; I knew something else was wrong.

It transpired that they had been upping his medication, and this was the effect of too much.

'Chlorpromazine.'

It was a drug I had come across in my studies, a powerful antipsychotic used to sedate disturbed patients. I couldn't believe they had been dosing him up with such strong psychotropic medication, but the nurses said it was the only way he could be kept on the ward.

When we went home that evening, we all sat round the kitchen table. Mother was sobbing, and Artie was beside himself.

"We have to get him out of there," he said

And we did.

We contacted the hospital and, after a lot of persuasion on my part, they agreed that we could bring Isaac back home. In the end, they relented as hospital beds were precious, and they had plenty of other candidates for poor Isaac's place.

Isaac came home, and between us, we endeavoured to look after him as best we could.

It was then that our luck changed a bit. The area where we lived had a centre nearby where "handicapped teenagers" were sent instead of mainstream school. This "training centre" was called Fieldways . After many letters and phone calls, we managed to get a place for Isaac, and a big bus arrived each morning to take him to his new "school." A doctor in the centre prescribed Thyroxine for Isaac, the hormone treatment for his low functioning gland, and his behavior and weight started to improve.

For a few years, Isaac settled and seemed to thrive on the routine of the centre and its dedicated staff. He learned Scottish country dancing and soon was able to do simple reels. This gave him immense pleasure. He would try to dance at every opportunity.

One year, there was a little Christmas display at the centre, and Isaac was the star, dancing with his partner Emily, who also had Down syndrome. They both loved Christmas, and that year, a kindly father of one of the handicapped children had dressed up as Santa and distributed some presents brought by the council. It was a happy time for the few simple souls that attended the centre. The staff members were kind and loving, and we hoped that this oasis for Isaac and his little friends would never dry up.

Sadly, this was not to be, and the council became short of money. It was decided by some committee or other that the centre would have to close. The nearest alternative was now some 50 miles away in a forest, virtually cut off from civilization and almost impossible to get to. Isaac was offered a place and went there for a few weeks, but once again, the disruption to his settled routine caused behavioural problems. After a few days, it was apparent that this solution was not going to work. The staff said with regret that they could not care for him there unless he was sedated, so Isaac stayed at home again.

My brother, mother, and I coped as best we could. At least it was better than having him froth at the mouth and drugged up to his eyes.

A letter arrived one morning. My father had sent a cheque and had told the bank to send one each month until I finished my studies. I was surprised but not unhappy, rationalizing it as something that was owed to the family for my father's behavior.

I was 18, and I had determined to get into university.

And I did.

I had been doing well and had obtained an interview for a teaching hospital to do medicine. I had talked for a long time at the interview about my reasons for taking this career course and about Down syndrome, a subject on which I was now a bit of an expert. It had procured me the offer of a place.

I managed reasonable grades in my exams, although not as good as they should have been and was due to start my studies later that year.

Isaac got worse.

We had stopped the alternative medication the doctor prescribed to subdue him, and Artie and I helped look after Isaac when he had tantrums or upsets; these had virtually ceased, but now he became physically unwell. He started to lose weight and seemed to choke on his food. The doctor came and duly sent him for some tests at the hospital, but he was uncooperative, and the tests couldn't be completed. Mother wanted him to stay at home, so I commuted to university to do my studies and lived at home to be with them. This caused a lot of tension, and it was clear that we were all walking around on eggshells, building up stress and tension within the home. I would go off and play football, but Mother had no such release and Artie was struggling with being a teenager himself. I was sure he was experimenting with drugs, maybe just weed, and I was sure he smoked. I just hoped he would come through that phase. I didn't have the energy to berate him, and perhaps it was his release too.

We managed, but Isaac was deteriorating, and often just lay on his bed. All the dancing and liveliness seemed to have gone.

One day Isaac started choking on his food again and went blue.

My mother called for an ambulance, and he was taken to the local hospital.

When I arrived later that afternoon, I rushed to the ward where they had taken Isaac. Mother and Artie were there, and Isaac lay on his bed lifeless and looking very pale.

"What is it?" I asked

"We don't know. The doctor's coming when he can, they said," my poor mother sobbed, obviously thinking the worst.

We sat and sat, and eventually, I got up and went to the nurses' station.

"I'm sorry to trouble you, but does anyone know anything about Isaac Galley, please?"

A man in a white coat, a doctor, turned his head.

"Young chap with Down's?"

"Yes, that's right."

"Just got his bloods back, and you are…?"

"His brother. I'm a medical student."

"Ah, best come with me."

He ushered me into a side room and sat me down. He stood over me while he told me Isaac had leukaemia, and there "wasn't much they could do."

"Sorry old chap."

And he left.

I must have sat there for some time. The sterile room and clean walls were a fitting backdrop for this news: cold, unemotional, matter of fact. I never imagined a time when Isaac wouldn't be in our lives, and now I had to contemplate that very thought.

When I eventually went back to Isaac's bedside, Mother was looking happier.

"He's a bit better, look. The nurse says he can have some tea soon, just mushed up so he doesn't choke again."

"Gorse," said Isaac – that's what he called me, as he couldn't say "George."
"Gorse – tea?"

I got up and turned towards the window

"Hey, let's get some tea, George," said Artie.

Artie had sensed that something was wrong, and his intuition, as usual, was correct. We walked off the ward and downstairs to where there was a little trolley shop.

We sat in the corridor with our tea.

"What is it, George?"

"I don't know how we're going to tell Mother," I said, "but Isaac has leukaemia"

"Can't they cure that nowadays?"

"Maybe…"

"Sure they can! Or you'll find a cure yourself, clever old doctor!"

"Artie, its serious."

"He'll be alright, I know he will. You're always doom and gloom. You can see he looks better already. Come on, sup up! We'd best be taking Mum a cuppa."

Artie didn't get it. Life was always going to be all right in his eyes, whatever happened. Couldn't keep him down. Even when it was obvious he was wrong, he'd just smile and shrug it off.

But that wouldn't work this time.

Isaac stayed in the hospital, and Mum went to visit every day. He didn't get better; he didn't get worse. After a few weeks, the doctor called Mother into his office. He explained that although Isaac was stable, he was too weak to come home, and the best place for him would be a nursing home. He recommended one out in the country.

"Good fresh air, good food. He'll be quite happy there."

Mother had no choice but to agree, but the home was over 100 miles away, and we had no transport.

Mother, Artie, and I were sitting in her front parlour. Mother told us that she had decided to move to be closer to Isaac.

"That's fine, Mum," said Artie. "I knew things would work out. I've just been accepted into the army, so you can sell up here, and get a nice little cottage near Isaac."

"What do you mean, army!" I shouted.

"Steady on there. It's a good job, well paid, and I'll get Christmas off this year."

"But Artie, there's a war in Vietnam…"

"We won't get involved. Don't worry, just a storm in a teacup."

I was very afraid that Artie didn't know what he was letting himself in for. But he was determined, and it did mean he would be self-sufficient. He'd left school at 16 with no qualifications. He'd gone after so many jobs and had always been rejected.

"I suppose you're right."

"Never thought I'd hear you say that!"

Mother managed to sell the house, not for a great profit, but enough to buy a little cottage just five miles from the ancient nursing home that Isaac was moved to. I visited it with her before going back to medical school. The building was old and draughty but the rooms were reasonably comfortable, and for the first time, I didn't feel that Isaac was a complete outsider. There were two other chaps with Down syndrome there, and they went off each day to a small farm nearby where they were given simple tasks. Isaac wasn't strong enough for that, but it was a goal that the family could aim for. Isaac's leukemia seemed to be quiescent. and his strength slowly improving. Things were perhaps looking up…

Maybe Artie was right after all.

5
Charles, 1875-1938

I am an artist, first and foremost. I have always wanted to paint, landscapes, seascapes, pictures of great imagination…

But I was forced to do portraits for the money, not because of anything to do with art. I was able to create a perfect likeness, and so my clients loved me for it, perfect in as much as I ironed out those little flaws that they didn't want to see, a mole here, a crooked nose there. They were surreptitiously removed. It never ceased to please. The people saw what they wanted to see in their portraits. No one really saw my great works though; I kept them hidden, like I did so much of my life.

I truly only wanted to be left alone to paint and to experience that inner exhilaration when a canvass leapt back out at you and sang: sang of the sweat and toil and love that went into its being; the fine brush strokes, the glorious colours and hues, the atmosphere.

But no, it was portraits; portraits of the vain, the overindulged, and the hypocrites that swarmed to my studio when I was in fashion and kept well away when I was not. I was told I was good looking, but when I looked in the mirror, I only saw ugliness. There was tarnish on my soul, and I could not paint over it or drink it away; although I certainly tried my best to do so.

I was best left alone to paint and later to drink. Brandy, that tonic, that lifesaver. How it blotted out reality, like a brush full of thick oil paint smeared on a canvas glossing over all that festered beneath it. It did its job, brandy did, and I let it.

What had made me like this, you ask? Prejudice, discrimination, hatred – yes, all those things, but mainly cowardice. I was a coward, in many senses of the word. I was not true to myself, and therefore, not to my family or my country.

It all started well enough; a comfortable boyhood, a good education, money. I was allowed to pursue my chosen career as long as I married well. That was the deal.

I was introduced to Mary at a small gathering in London. I had been invited by some of my society friends, and my father had established that Mary would be there with her chaperone. My father had already determined that I should marry her, as she was, of course, an heiress and a beauty. What more could I have wanted? She was, indeed, pleasant enough and made the right utterances about my work, was attentive but not overbearing, and undeniably good to look at. She was the youngest daughter, the two elder sisters being far too old now to attract a suitable male. Neither had Mary's looks or charm, and they fussed around her like besotted mother hens. Their father was pinning all his hopes of a decent match on Mary and had settled a fortune on her. He had escorted her from the family home in Germany to make a good solid English marriage. And I was the talk of the town, the most eligible bachelor. Artists were in fashion or were not. I was in, having had a number of influential commissions, and unabashedly, I enjoyed the attention.

My father encouraged me in my courtship, which was superficial and meaningless in my eyes. Mary seemed willing and so, after the appropriate time, I went to her father, who was soon to return to Germany, and asked for Mary's hand. I didn't realize then that he was a Jew. Both families were delighted at the engagement, far more so than the couple themselves.

And so, on a dull May morning, we attended the large parish church and were blessed in holy matrimony. Her mother and father did not attend, pleading illness and an inability to partake of the long journey, but I sensed that they were ashamed of their true religion and wanted Mary to escape from the prejudice and stigma of being Jewish. Mary never showed any signs of religious tendency and never mentioned her background. My parents never enquired.

We were to stay on our wedding night at a scrumptious hotel and occupied the bridal suite. We dined together that evening and prepared to retire for the night. I had consumed plenty of brandy, enough, I hoped, that I could do my duty.

Once in the bedchamber, I quickly took off my wedding attire and awaited my bride. She modestly slipped into the large four-poster bed and lay perfectly still.

I willed my body to perform but, as usual, there was little response. My wife no doubt blamed the brandy and was probably not that interested.

The next morning, we lay side by side, not speaking. I grabbed at myself and as quickly as I could, pulled my new bride into position.

That brief perfunctory liaison resulted in our first daughter. I did not go near my wife again, and as she was so quickly pregnant, no one thought any more of it.

Amelia was born, and we lived with adequate help in my studios in London. We continued the pretense of married life, and when Amelia was two years old, my wife came to my rooms.

"I want another child," she told me flatly. "My father wants us to have a son, and we are more than dependent on his money, as you know. I want you to understand, it is not my idea."

That night, having charged myself with brandy, I reluctantly managed to perform my duty once again. It was quick and messy, and I left the bedchamber immediately after. Some weeks later, I was informed that my wife was pregnant. I breathed a huge sigh of relief and continued to collect commissions for my work. There was no shortage of funds, and when the boy was born, I knew that the money fountain would not dry up just yet. My father-in-law had his wish. A rich Jew, he tried to pull the family's strings from afar, but his wealth lay in Germany, and he had decided it was better to live there – a decision he later regretted. His saving grace was that he was besotted with his daughter and granted her every wish. In return, she produced the son and heir he hoped for, and he poured money into her whims and wants, including a mansion in Sussex. I still needed to have some money for myself, so that I could secret myself away from prying eyes and whispers, so I did what was required and did not speak of it.

After a while though, I started to feel resentful of portrait painting and decided to only agree to the occasional client. The rest of the time I spent in my club with my friend the brandy bottle. There was a young steward who would always attend me there. He had beautiful brown eyes and smiled deeply at me every evening as I arrived. Sometimes, he would brush past me as he served me, and I could feel electricity as our skin touched. We chatted. At first, it was harmless banter, but soon, I was seeking him out after his work and lingering with a cigarette in my hand, by the tradesmen's entrance.

One evening, when I knew my wife was at her father's house in Sussex for a few days, I invited him back to my studio. I told him I would like to paint his portrait, and he jumped at the chance. He sat perfectly still while I started my initial sketches.

"It may be better if you take off your jacket and tie."

He did so, and I felt that electricity again. An hour passed, and he got up to leave.

"Got to be at work early, sir." He grinned and held out his hand. I placed a guinea note in it.

"Tomorrow?" I asked

"Sure," he said.

I spent all night looking at the portrait I had started and fussed over it till morning. I slept for most of the day but raised myself by six o'clock in the evening and took vast time and trouble over my appearance. I doused myself in cologne and brushed and re-brushed my hair.

I waited outside the club until 11 p.m. and watched the young man as he jumped down the steps onto the pavement beside me.

"Shall we?" He grinned.

We strolled back to the studio, and he proceeded to take off his jacket and tie. This time he also took off his shirt.

I think he heard my audible gasp as he said, "Is this alright?"

With trembling hands, I tried to paint and sketch, but it was no use. I walked over to him and put my hand on his shoulder.

"Could you turn just a little this way?"

My hand followed the contours of his skin and onto his neck and face. I was gazing at him in a trance.

"What on Earth…?"

I turned quickly to see Mary in her coat and hat. She had returned unexpectedly and very late from the country, and must have heard our voices.

"You'd better go," I whispered to the boy, and he hurriedly dressed and scooped up the guinea that was on the sideboard.

Nothing was ever said, but she knew.

We continued our sham of a marriage. Mary spent more and more time at the house in Sussex. I'm sure she had affairs, and I couldn't blame her. I couldn't give her what she wanted physically. I know she grew to detest me, and she also grew very cold with the children. It was as if she was punishing them for being mine. I never acted on my attractions, preferring instead to paint them. Anyone looking at my portfolio might have commented on the number of handsome young men that had had their portraits painted by me. Years passed.

Then came war. I couldn't fight. I was terrified of physical harm and of deprivation. I was a sensitive and selfish being, needing to be cosseted and looked after, and the stories of the trenches made my stomach turn. I couldn't believe it when Arthur told me he was going to join up. I know he was trying to be the man I never was. I should have stopped him, but I was in a state of stupor. Brandy and self-loathing had consumed my mind.

Years later, Mary came to me and told me I was to do one last thing for her. She was pregnant and wanted the child to remain with Amelia and me in London. She never told me who the father was, but I guessed it was probably that American Major she often sought out in New York on her "business" trips. I argued against the arrangement but knew I owed it to her. I had never wanted for money because of her father and her inheritance. My commissions weren't enough to keep me in brandy.

And so, the baby George stayed here, poor boy. His mother disowned him, his sister chastised him, and his father ignored him. His biological father was in America, and I'm not even sure if he knew of George's existence.

But, true to my cowardly nature, I kept quiet, painted pictures of my beautiful boys, and drank Mary's finest brandy. Then the money stopped. I suspected Mary's finances had dipped and she was no longer able to keep me as well. Amelia held the household together as best she could. We had to let all the servants go, and the house decayed under our very noses. My drinking increased, and I would loiter around clubs with a brandy bottle in my hand until the early hours. The police got to know me well, and a couple of kindly coppers would often bring me home to Amelia. For some reason, she stayed with me.

I am lying in the gutter again with a smashed brandy bottle nearby. Somehow, I think this will be the last time.

6
Artie, 1956-1968

I don't know when it first started, perhaps when Dad left, but my mind would often go into a sort of overdrive. I could see things so clearly. Patterns would sort of come out of nowhere, and that would make sense of everything, as if it was all connected.

Colours would have different meanings and come together in perfect matches. I knew that everything was fantastic, special. I was special, and we were all special. Sometimes, my mind would race so quickly that I couldn't get my words out straight. They'd tumble out in a jumble of alien sounds, which made me laugh.

It became much more difficult to control when I started at the barracks. I wasn't badly treated, but there were written instructions and tests and often I couldn't make sense of them. I fell behind and was put on extra duties. I didn't feel stressed, but I suppose I must have been. My mates were good to me and tried to bail me out. I got stuck with a rather strict sergeant-major (yes, I know they're all supposed to be strict!), but this one had it in for me.

One night, after lights out, I just couldn't sleep. My mind was racing again, and this time, I couldn't control it. I felt very hot, so I took off all my clothes. The clock in the dorm was telling me to sing, so I started to belt out an old nursery rhyme.

"Ride a cock horse to Banbury cross…" I thought it was funny. "A cock horse," what did that mean? I giggled.

"Oi, mate, what the hell do you think you're doing?"

I guess I heard him at some level, but not really, and I kept on singing.

"To see a fine lady upon a white horse…" I laughed because it sounded so poncy. It was an amazing feeling to be so high, like I was on top of the world.

"You been on drugs or something?"

"Artie! Put your clothes on!"

I could hear them all in the background, but I didn't have time to pay any attention.

One of the squaddies tried to get me to put my shirt on, but I didn't want to stop singing, as it made me feel so good. He came too near, so I pushed him away. It was quite a hard push and he fell backwards, though I didn't mean to hurt him. Two other squaddies then tried to pin me down, but I felt I had the strength of an ox and threw them off with ease.

"He's gone bonkers – get the sarge!"

"If the sarge sees him like this, Lord knows what he'll do! Are you sure he's not been on something?"

"Like what?"

I laughed at the voices that sounded so worried.

"Chill out," I said in my mind, or was it out loud? By then everything had sort of merged together.

Meanwhile, I started to climb up towards a high window as my singing gave me more strength. I knew I could fly and wanted to soar out into the night air.

"For God's sake, someone stop him!"

One of the soldiers must have run out to the nearest telephone box and phoned George. They all knew George was a medical student and had his number from when we'd all had a beer together a few weeks back.

The lads pinned me down and stopped me "flying," but I wasn't having any of it. I think I hit one of them, didn't mean to, but he got in my way and didn't realize how important I was, I couldn't blame him. He clearly wasn't "in the know."

Then, the squaddies kept me on my bed and held me firm. I started to relax and slumped into a stupor. Inside my head though, everything was going at full speed, thousands of faces, sounds, colours, emotions jangled through my brain like rocket fuel.

"Artie? Artie, it's me, George. What on Earth are you doing?"

I vaguely heard George's voice.

"Blue is yellow, yellow is green, one, three, five…" I said again; I was sure George would understand me.

"What are you talking about? Has anyone given you anything?"

"Blue is yellow…" I could see George, but no one else, George would understand; he would know what I meant.

Suddenly the sergeant-major came in to the dorm, and I saw him out of the corner of my eye. He was the Joker, a fool!

"What on Earth is all this? Galley, what the hell do you think you're doing?"

"I'm sorry, sir. I'm his brother; I think he's unwell," I heard George say in the background, and it made me smile. George knew I was all-powerful, so he was clearly trying to put the sergeant off the scent. Clever.

"What do you mean? He looks like he's acting crazy!"

Haha, crazy… eh?, so wrong, so wrong.

"Um, er, it's a fever, delirium or something. I'm a medical student. I'll take him."

I suspect George tried to come up with something that wouldn't ruin my chances in the army. They were so po-faced! The squaddies were alright though.

"Sick in the head! Get him out of here and to a hospital! Can't have this here. Jameson, get a jeep, take Galley and his brother to the emergency clinic."

I didn't want to go anywhere, but I knew George would look after me, and then, when we escaped, I could teach him how to fly, it was so easy…

7
George, 1968

Artie was quite compliant with me, but he kept smiling in a conspiratorial way. His broad frame and strong arms bared to the world, he looked like a colossus in battle with the Greek gods. His short red hair roamed unruly about his head and his green eyes were fiery with madness. He was a good-looking man with a square chin and strong features. As I looked at him, I couldn't understand what had happened to this gentle giant. I hoped to goodness that the occasional dabble with weed hadn't turned into something more sinister.

The jeep arrived, and we managed to get Artie into it, wrapped in a blanket. He sat rocking back and forth and grinning with the occasional snigger, and when he looked at me, he winked in a funny sequence. I couldn't quite make out what this conspiratorial winking was, but I was glad that Artie had calmed down and thankful he didn't try to escape. Jameson drove us the 10 or so miles to the emergency department of the local hospital. We waited for two hours with Artie trying to get up and fly every so often. It took all my powers of persuasion to keep him in the waiting area.

Eventually, we were seen by a doctor and not before time! Artie was revving up and stood by the window in the doctor's office as he started to disrobe again. I explained to the doctor that I was a medical student.

"What do you make of his behavior? Ever seen him like this before?"

"No, he's usually very happy go lucky, easy sort of bloke"

"Do you think he's taken anything?"

"Not wittingly." I didn't dare mention cannabis, but I was pretty sure this wasn't down to a bit of puffing.

"Well, he hasn't got a fever or anything overtly medical, looks like some sort of breakdown, I'll get the liaison psychiatrist to come and see him"

After another two hours, a rather sunken-eyed doctor with a wispy beard came into the room. I had managed to keep Artie relatively quiet by listening to his mumbo jumbo and repeating it back to him, but he was beginning to rev up yet again.

The young doctor started to ask questions, and Artie's eyes glazed over. He had started his chanting and gobbledygook again. I tried to answer as best I could on Artie's behalf, but now, Artie was becoming quite agitated.

"I think we'll have to sedate him."

Artie was strong, and even I was having difficulty holding him.

The doctor disappeared and then returned with two burly charge nurses and a large syringe.

"Chlorpromazine."

My heart sank. They obviously thought Artie had had a major psychotic problem, as this was a drug used in only the most serious of psychiatric cases, and of course with Isaac.

"Mr. Galley, I want to give you an injection to calm you down."

"Blue, blue, yellow, blue, you know, you know."

"Hold him, please."

"Come on, Artie, this will help you. Don't pull away now, come on."

Artie thumped me in the chest, whereupon the two burly nurses grabbed his arms and wispy beard jabbed him quickly in his bare buttock.

Half an hour later, Artie was strapped to the bed and snoring loudly. The doctor took me into a dingy little office and sat me down.

"We're going to have to do a Mental Health section on your brother, I'm afraid. It would appear he has had a major psychotic breakdown, and we'll need to monitor and treat him. I've taken a series of blood tests including drug screen, but I don't think this is narcotic induced. In my experience, this is likely to be a manic episode, or the beginnings of schizophrenia; his premorbid personality from what you tell me would suggest the former, but we will need a whole lot more observation time before a full diagnosis can be made. Now, it would help us immensely if you would sign the section papers, so we can act quickly and get to the bottom of this."

My world was collapsing around my ears.

"In his experience…" What was he, 20? But I knew, in the logical part of my brain, that he was right. There was no other explanation, and Artie would never consent to treatment in his present state. The doctor used lots of medical jargon thinking I would understand it, but the words "mania" and "schizophrenia" drummed through my brain, both a life sentence.

"Okay." I said, gingerly. "Where will he go?"

"St. Austin's, nearby psychiatric hospital."

Or "Hell," as it was known locally.

I knew enough about these places from my classmates at medical school. One or two had had placements to the wards at St. Austin's as part of their psychiatry training. Each of us had to spend two weeks at a psychiatric hospital and get signed up before being eligible to take our final medical exams. The wards were full of strange and unhappy people, and the psychiatric nurses had their hands full trying to keep order on the wards. Some patients were on suicide watch, and others just sat and chain-smoked, rocking back and forth in a mesmerizing way. The two conditions that wispy beard had suggested filled me with dread. Both were chronic major illnesses, and the poor sufferers of these conditions often spent their lives revolving back and forth onto psychiatric wards with delusions, hallucinations, and crazed hyperactivities.

Artie was going to be sent to such a ward, and I nearly cried.

At first, Artie was heavily sedated, like all his fellow inmates, but after a few days, they reduced the doses, and Artie started to emerge from the alter-ego that he had developed. Back, I hoped, to the Artie that I knew.

I realised that Artie needed help, but it just didn't feel right. The hospital was a stark grey building, surrounded by high walls and no foliage to speak of in the grounds. It was as if this barren environment was a result of years of troubled minds being contained in whatever way was possible. There was no time or inclination for colour or art. It was a clinical, cold place, full of cigarette smoke and jangling keys that locked each of the ward and staffroom doors, a prison; incarceration.

"George, mate, you've got to get me out of here."

I was visiting Artie, as I had done every evening after studies.

"How are you feeling?"

"I'm great, but I can't stay here now. Every night, they scream, and this old bloke in the next bed keeps trying to climb into my bed with me. I had to push him off last night, and he fell on the floor. Poor sod doesn't know what he's doing."

"They won't take you back into the army until you've passed the medical, and you're still on medication," I tried to argue.

"No, I'm not," said Artie and produced a handful of large red pills. "Not taking them."

He grinned.

"But you'll relapse, Artie, you were really sick!"

"No, I was just a bit revved up, that's all. The pills give me a horrendous hangover, and I can't think at all when I take them. I'm fine now. Look, I know you can get me out, just sign some papers or something."

I couldn't help but agree that the patients were treated like animals, and so most of them end up behaving like animals.

"I'm writing it all down," Artie said, and I saw a pile of scribbles next to his bed.

I looked at Artie. He seemed fine again, but I could still detect a brittleness that had clearly been part of what was now evidently a manic episode. He was right though. This hospital was no therapeutic environment, and I couldn't see how anyone could ever get better in these circumstances. I had looked up mania, and there was a chance it was just a one-off episode, a stress reaction, but there was also more of a possibility that Artie was suffering from a bipolar disorder, manic depression.

"Look, I'll speak to the doctor. Just give it a couple more days till you're strong again. All this sleep deprivation can't be doing you any good."

"I'm fine George, I want to come home with you now. I'll tell the army I just had a bit of a funny turn. They'll be okay."

I went off to try and find the duty doctor while Artie started to pack his things up. While I was away, a nurse had asked Artie what he was doing. When I came back from unsuccessfully trying to find the doctor there were three nurses around Artie's bed, and he was being manhandled to the ground. Wispy beard appeared as if from nowhere and another large syringe was brandished in Artie's direction

"What are you doing? He was fine just a moment ago!"

"He's trying to abscond," said one of the nurses.

"George, George, get them off me! We're the superheroes! We can fly away!"

"Artie, calm down, man! Don't do that!"

But it was all too late. The stash of red pills had been found, and wispy beard jabbed his large hypodermic into Artie's thigh through his pyjama trousers. Soon, they had Artie strapped down, and he was becoming drowsy again.

"Can I have a word?"

Wispy beard escorted me off to his dingy office.

"Look, I'm terribly sorry, but your brother really is very ill. He's manipulative and difficult and won't take his medication."

"But he says it makes him feel dreadful."

"Yes, we are aware there can be some side effects, but without it, his psychosis takes over, and he's a danger to himself and everyone else. We're going to have to put him on special observation and keep him here for the foreseeable future. I'm very sorry, but he's under a Mental Health Section, and we have a duty."

"Couldn't you change the medication?"

"Perhaps when he's a bit more stable, but as he's been hiding the medication we've been giving him, he'll have to have injections now."

With an extremely heavy heart, I trundled away from St. Austin's. I decided not to visit Artie for a while. It was too distressing, and I think I made Artie feel he could "beat the system" by being his brother and "almost" a doctor.

Many days passed, and eventually, I plucked up courage to go back to the ward.

I managed to locate Artie, who was now in a small room with a nurse outside his door.

I went in and couldn't believe my eyes. Artie was a shadow, sunken eyed and stubbly chin. He hardly moved and sat by the window staring into space. An ashtray piled high with stubs sat by his bed.

"Artie?"

He turned slowly, his face a hollowed-out greyness.

"Umm…"

"How are you, mate?"

Artie didn't respond but turned to stare out of the window. What had happened to him? There was no spark, no Artie left at all.

I rushed to speak with the doctor and demanded an audience with someone – now. Eventually, after a lot of arguing (I was very polite, but firm, and they got the message that I wasn't leaving!), I was shown into a reasonable office with a large desk.

The door opened and a man in his late fifties with greying, longish hair and a cardigan hanging over his shoulders came in. He shook me warmly by the hand and introduced himself as Dr. O'Donnelly.

"Galley, isn't it? You're a med student, I believe. How's it going? Tough in this day and age, isn't it?

"Now, about your brother Artie. Rotten luck. I'm sure we can help, but I need to get him down to my unit in Kent, you'd be okay with that, wouldn't you? Treat mainly medical staff, but as he's a relative of a medic, I'm sure we can swing it."

I must have sat with my mouth open. I was completely taken aback by this warm, friendly Irishman.

It transpired that Dr. O'Donnelly went around the psychiatric wards in the area picking patients whom he thought he could help with new methods. Talking therapies, lighter medications, better trained staff, one-to-one treatments. It was all a bit experimental, and he chose mainly afflicted medical staff to work with. I was happy that Artie might have a route out of St. Austin's and agreed immediately to his transfer.

That turned out to be one of the best things I ever did for Artie. Within months, he was back to his old self and had some insights into what made his mind race and how to prevent relapses. But the army wouldn't take him back, so he became reliant on benefits. He lived in a hostel once he was discharged from Dr .O'Donnelly's care and desperately sought work. We started to lose contact as I became busier and busier with my studies, and he distanced himself from the family. My mother and Isaac lived nearby, and he managed to visit them every month. But his lack of employment was becoming an issue.

Meanwhile, I had to knuckle down to my studies if I was to pass my finals and get house jobs in the local hospital. I knew I was behind in my work. It was so hard to study and live at the same time. I knew this was something I had to get to grips with, as life was never going to go away, and neither was work.

I had a room in a student house not far from the hospital. It was basic but did the job. I had a desk with some drawers and an angle poise lamp that I picked up at a junk shop. Much of what was in the flat was from junk shops as well, and I only hoped the lifestyle of a fully qualified doctor was better than this. The old bed I slept in was musty, and I don't think I helped myself by regularly forgetting to change the sheets. I now had six months to get my studies in order, and I started hitting the books with a vengeance. Something always distracted me though, and in particular there was a problem brewing with one of the charge nurses in Casualty. He was an arrogant bloke, and I believed he was unhappy that his badge read "nurse" and not "doctor." He decided to take it out on me. I had been assigned to Casualty for the six weeks leading up to the exams and usually these last placements were token, as the wards and staff knew we medical students were studying for finals. I arrived in Casualty, donned my short white student coat, and made myself available for any jobs that might need doing, while attaching myself to the Registrar, who said he would call me for interesting patients to practice my consultation skills on. The charge nurse collared me each day as soon as I arrived and had me doing basic dressings and suturing. I was happy to do this, but he never let up on me for a moment, even though all the other students had breaks.

After a week of relentless bullying, I decided to have a word with him. Well, that was a mistake. I asked him politely if it would be possible to ease up just a little on the tasks so I could attend the Registrar's teaching and get away before midnight. He went into a flat spin and told me how over-privileged and lazy I was. I was happy to take some of his vitriol, but this seemed completely out of proportion to anything I might have done to upset him.

Things boiled over, and I stormed off out of his office and outside into the nearby ambulance bay. I wasn't going to take anymore and had told him so. The next thing I knew, he was following me and was lining up a right hook. A passing ambulance driver cottoned on quickly and stood in front of me to stop him. The right hook landed on this chap's shoulder, who then grabbed the charge nurse and arm-wrestled him to the floor.

"Oi, mate, what the hell do you think you're doing!"

The driver released the charge nurse, who brushed past me, back inside.

"What the hell was all that about?" he asked

"Damned if I know," I said.

"Charlie's got a pretty short fuse, especially since his partner's been diagnosed with AIDS," the ambulance driver told me.

"Good grief, I had no idea."

"Best avoid him. He's clearly got it in for you."

AIDS. This was a new and devastating problem sweeping through the clandestine homosexual community, and something we were only just beginning to learn about. I hurriedly left Casualty and headed back to my room. I opened my textbooks and devoured the chapter on deficiency in the immune system and the HIV virus.

I steered clear of that Charge nurse, understanding, I thought, a little more about why he might have gone for me. One of the female nurses took me aside and told me I bore a remarkable resemblance to the charge nurse's partner. I didn't know how I could have helped that, but at least it made more sense now. I was alive and kicking while his poor partner was slowly and painfully dying.

The whole incident galvanized me into more studying, until I felt reasonably prepared. The final exams arrived.

They seemed to go on forever, even though it was only a week. Two papers a day and then oral exams and practical tests. I finally returned home, finished and spent, and flopped onto my unmade bed. I think I must have slept for 14 hours.

A few days later, the results were due, and I went to the medical school notice board milling around with all the other expectant students. The results were up. Mostly there were smiles and whoops of joy; an occasional student slunk away with an obvious fail. I looked for my name.

Galley, G. Pass

*

Life as a newly qualified doctor was hard but rewarding. Our white coats and stethoscopes imbued a certain heroic character upon us, and patients and staff were deferential and polite. The hours were long, and sometimes, we would not go to bed at all on a busy weekend on duty. The doctors' mess was a sanctuary, and we had good food and booze on tap. Very few of us actually drank when we were on duty, but some of the rugby-playing surgeons (or should I say surgical rugby players!) could sink a few and still manage to work.

There was one chap, name of Dr. Neil Smith, who was clearly having problems, and each of us prayed that we wouldn't be on duty with him. He had managed to become a medical registrar in spite of his drinking. When sober, he was a nice enough chap, but in his cups, he became loud and unpredictable.

One night, we admitted a boy with Down syndrome with a severe infection. The patient was a young adult, severely short of breath and beginning to turn a tinge of blue (called cyanosis) due to lack of oxygen. I was on duty with Neil, took a medical history from the boy's mother, and went off to fetch equipment to put up a drip and administer intravenous antibiotics. I asked the nurses to fetch oxygen meantime. When I came back, there was no sign of the boy in the cubicle. I went to the nurses' station and asked what had happened.

"Dr. Smith's orders, Dr. Galley. No treatment, just TLC."

I couldn't believe it. "TLC" meant "tender loving care," but also certain death if this boy didn't get treatment quickly.

"Where's Dr. Smith?"

"Not sure, Dr. Galley, probably up in the bar by now," smirked the nurse. They were all well aware of Dr. Smith, but no one did anything about his behavior.

I raced off towards the doctor's mess, but before I could get there, an alarm sounded. An elderly patient was having a cardiac arrest, and so, I had to divert to attend, as I was the house officer on duty.

We spent an hour or so trying to save the poor soul, but sadly failed. The patient was frail and had heart failure and diabetes. It was not a real surprise that he died. The anesthetist on duty had to lead the resuscitation attempt, as there was no sign of Dr. Smith. Once we had sorted out the arrangements for the deceased patient and spoken to the relatives, another couple of hours had passed.

I rushed up to the doctor's mess once more, but couldn't find Dr. Smith. I banged on his door, but there was no answer. Eventually, I gave up and walked down to the wards to see if I could find the boy with Down syndrome. On the second medical ward I went to, I saw curtains pulled around a bed in the middle. I went over and looked inside. There was the Down's boy with his mother at his bedside.

"He died peacefully, like Dr. Smith said he would," the mother told me through her tears, in a very resigned way.

"I'm so sorry," I managed to blurt out. "I'll leave you together"

I drew the curtains quickly and left. So many emotions were running through me. I was angry, sad, frustrated, and guilty and a whole lot more.

The anesthetist was in the office as I passed.

"Shame about the Down's lad, had intractable heart failure, and that infection just sent him over the top."

"Surely if he'd had intravenous antibiotics?"

"Says here that he was really needle-phobic, and that his heart was on its last legs."

The old notes for the patient had arrived on the ward. I hadn't seen them when I clerked the boy in.

"So... do you think it was inevitable then?"

"Who knows, but on balance it was probably better to let him die peacefully if his time was up."

I was so confused. Was it ethical that we withheld treatment? Could we have saved him? Would the distress of having an intravenous line shoved into him have speeded his demise? Would his heart have given up soon anyway?

My head was spinning, and I realised I hadn't had any sleep for over 24 hours.

"Where's that Dr. Smith then?" asked the anesthetist. "Should really have been at that cardiac arrest," he mumbled.

At that, his bleep went off again, and he got up to leave.

"Go and get some rest old chap, all seems quiet now"

I went back up to the mess and towards the on-call room. As I went along the corridor, I saw Dr. Smith coming out of his room

"Down's boy snuffed it then," he breathed, and on his breath, I could smell alcohol.

"Where were you?" I cried. "We had a patient with a cardiac arrest."

"Old bloke on ward 8? No point in thumping on *his* chest."

Dr. Smith slightly wobbled and tottered off down the corridor.

Words failed me, and I stormed away.

I later discovered that Dr. Smith had been diagnosed with a rare cancer and, a few months later, was dead himself. I remembered a lesson from my medical student days: "Assume nothing."

I had assumed Dr. Smith was a write-off, a drunk, and a sot, but he was actually dealing with his own hell.

I tried to make sense of everything that had happened and particularly in the context of my own family. There were so many questions and very few answers, but I did learn that everything was not always what it first seemed at face value. There were reasons why things happened and why people reacted the way they did. I determined to be a thorough and competent doctor, as best I could be. I also didn't want anyone who looked after patients with Down syndrome to write them off at first meeting.

8
Isaac, 1956-1972

Hello, my name is Isaac, but I can't say it. I can say Zackie. I can't speak properly or tell you how I feel, so I have to show you. I do that by dancing when I'm happy, or not moving when I'm sad, and saying "No." I used to be able to dance a lot, but I can't now.

I can say "yeah" and "no," and it means I like something or I don't.

I don't understand how the world works, but I like things the same, and I like my routine.

I don't know what a Mongol is, but I think I am one.

I don't have a good memory for things, but I can remember feelings. I remember happy feelings when I was little, but also scared feelings. Mama and Ardie and Gorse looked after me when I was smaller, and I remember feeling loved and safe. Sometimes, I would feel worried, as if something bad was going to happen. I got these feelings when something new or different happened. I didn't like it when things changed. I felt happy when I was with Emily and when we were dancing. I remembered the steps, although I didn't really think about them, they just happened. I like music and Christmas songs. I loved Emily. I liked to kiss her, but they wouldn't let me and smacked me. Emily and I would eat crisps together after dancing, and I would feed them into her mouth. It made us giggle.

Nowadays, I like to get up slowly, and I don't like it when they tell me to shower. I like sitting in a bath with Donald. Donald is a plastic duck, and he floats.

I like eggs and toast for breakfast, but I don't like to brush my teeth afterwards. I haven't got many teeth left now. My mouth often gets quite sore. I like to sit and watch TV, especially the news and *Top of the Pops*.

I like to listen to music and dance.

The people I know are Ardie and Gorse and Mama and Chrissie, who helps me. I don't know where Emily went. I don't see her anymore, and that makes me feel sad.

I love Father Christmas, although I'm not sure who he is or where he comes from. He brings presents at Christmas, and everyone seems happy when he's around. I'm not sure when Christmas is or what time it comes around, but I like it when it's happening.

Chrissie says Father Christmas lives at the North Pole, wherever that is. I don't think I want to live there because it sounds too cold. My hands go blue when it's cold.

Sometimes, Chrissie makes me go to the doctors, and I don't like that. I don't want them to put things on me, and I scream if I see a needle. I like to eat crisps and chicken and baked beans. They promise me those things if I'm good. I'm not quite sure what "good" is, but it usually involves me doing what I'm told and not necessarily what I want. This makes me feel upset, and I don't like that feeling.

I don't remember much clever stuff, but I can count to 10, sometimes. And I know some colours, especially purple.

I sometimes hit people. I don't mean to. I don't know how else to make them stop. I've learned some sign though. It's easier with Makaton. I think everybody should learn that.

I don't like things that move quickly. There's a cat that scares me because it runs across the room when I don't expect it. I'm okay with cuddly toys though.

I like to be dressed up warm, and I like my big bed and Ed. I don't know why I have to have blood tests, and I don't like them, but they put magic cream on my arm first. It still stings, and I pull my arm away. I used to have a lot more energy, but I just like to sit down now. I get a bit short of breath if I move around, and I sleep a lot. Some people look at me funny. They think I don't notice, but I do. I don't know what death is, but I've heard them whispering about it. My life is simple. I wake up, I eat, I try to smile. I am simple, not complicated. I like being simple. Life is simple really; I don't know why big people make it so complicated.

I think I want to go to sleep now.

*

George
1972

One day, Isaac didn't wake up. He died peacefully in his sleep in the home in the country where he had been since his diagnosis. I was called at 7 a.m. when Chrissie, his care giver, had gone in to get him up. He looked very peaceful laying in his big bed with Ed the teddy next to him. My mother broke down and wept inconsolably when I told her, and Artie came straight round from his hostel. We sat together for a while.

"We should tell father," Artie said.

No one answered. Mother said she would phone him later

"Do you have a number for him then?" I asked. It transpired that father had been keeping in touch with her ever since Isaac's diagnosis.

"He would want to know."

"We don't want to see him," I said.

"He has a right to come to the funeral," said Artie.

"How come you're so conciliatory?"

"That's a big word! Look, there's no point in being angry anymore. We have to accept Dad had his faults, but the most important thing is that Isaac had a good life as much as we could make it good for him, none of us is innocent or guilty, it's just how it is."

I cooled down and listened to my sensible, crazy brother. He had learned a lot from Dr. O'Donnelly, and not just about his own illness. He was a mature man now.

I had been sad to hear that Dr. O'Donnelly had retired, and it was rumored that his unit was shutting down. I hoped Artie was well enough to do without him now.

The funeral was difficult. There were only a few of us as we gathered at the crematorium on a beautiful autumnal morning. The colours of the trees in the garden of rest were yellow, ochre, and red, and a splendid light shone though the falling leaves, making a golden atmosphere. It was as though Isaac was smiling down on us, and it felt serene and peaceful.

Then, my father appeared, ghost like, silhouetted against the light. Artie moved slowly towards him and shook his hand and then walked away. I did the same, I think I saw a small tear in his eye – although it was very frosty and clear, which may have caused his eyes to water. Mother stood still. We then all walked into the chapel. There was a short eulogy by the local vicar who had known Isaac from his visits to the home. He spoke of love and happiness and simplicity of life – the things that we hoped Isaac had known in his short time on Earth. He didn't speak of discrimination, fear, and prejudice, which he had also known.

Isaac's coffin disappeared behind those awful curtains, which closed abruptly on a chapter of our lives. We now had to move forward and learn what we could from Isaac's life and passing.

After the funeral we gathered in a small hall next door where some kindly parishioners served hot tea and sandwiches. My father had disappeared, and in a way, I was glad I didn't have to speak to him. I suspect it was the decent thing to do, as it wasn't the occasion for scenes or retribution.

We gradually left one by one with tears in our eyes, back to reality.

My mother lost heart. With Isaac gone, her raison d'etre seemed to go also. She shuffled around her small cottage, and Artie and I visited when we could, but she was broken.

And then something strange happened.

My father returned from Brighton and went to live with mother in the cottage. He took the spare room, but he shopped and cleaned and cooked for Mother. I realised that she had become badly depressed and found out that she was on medication. Father had volunteered to come back to look after her, and he wrote to both Artie and I expressing his sorrow at what had happened before and how his own mental anguishes had stopped him from being a proper father to Isaac. However, he was better and stronger now and would make up as best he could by helping Mother in her despair and desperation.

It worked.

Within a year she was more like her old self. This was a great weight off my mind as I struggled to decide which pathway in a medical career I should take. I kept my distance but didn't feel that awful anger quite so much, and I hoped that perhaps now my parents could settle into some sort of happy existence.

9
Sally, 1916-1980

I think it's time I spoke up now. It hasn't been easy for me to do, as I am naturally quite shy and have been told that I don't have much self-esteem. I have been blessed though, with my boys and with Gee-O. No one really understood about Gee-O and me. I had fallen in love with him when he was such a young man. His fair wavy hair and hazel-green eyes, his slightly crooked nose, no doubt broken in some brawl as a kid, but for me, it was perfect. I'd never seen a man in that way before. He was at once strong and beautiful. I knew it would be difficult and that he never really felt the same way about me, but I hoped I could make him happy. People were so cruel when Gee-O left, all except Mrs. Joy, that is. I don't know what I would have done without her. People are so quick to judge and to jump to conclusions. When they attacked us with their harsh words and expressions, my eldest boy George could speak out from his brain and my middle boy Arthur from his heart, but my little Isaac spoke with his soul.

When I had Isaac, no one had heard of Down syndrome in my family. Later, I discovered that Gee-O, my husband, had read about it in a medical textbook, but we didn't really understand what it meant. We were not prepared for the prejudice and discrimination that having a different, simple child would bring. Gee-O couldn't cope. I know how he suffered with his nerves, but he never drank, and he never hit me. I couldn't reach out to him; I didn't have the words. I never really thought he left us, not completely. He just had to be away and let his own mind heal. He had been more damaged in the war than anyone ever realised, and his lack of love as a child made him distrustful and wary.

My father was so good to him and to me, but Dad didn't comprehend that a man could leave his family and still love them. The boys were so young, and I know they hated their father, especially George. Artie had a more tender soul, and I felt how he was torn in all directions when Gee-O left us. I think that affected his mind, too. I know Gee-o worked hard and didn't squander money. He sent as much as he could back to us. There was no fancy woman or lover in Brighton. I know that. I was happy enough. I knew I had always been lucky to marry Gee-O. He was nearly four years younger than me, and I was fast becoming "left on the shelf." I know my father pushed him a bit into proposing, but I had enough love for both of us.

Bringing up the boys was hard work, physically and emotionally. My neighbour, Mrs. Joy was a tower of strength in those days.

Not that she said very much other than, "there, there, dear… It'll be alright, you'll see," as she delivered another pie or loaf of bread made by her own hand. I never really had the time to find out much about her. She had always seemed to be there. I think her family came from Scotland, but I wasn't sure. She never had anyone visit, and she never went away. It was so sad when they took her off in an ambulance. I never did find out what happened. I must assume she died or went into a home.

But, of course, we had some good times, the boys and me. This was mainly because of Isaac. Although as a teenager, he was a bit of a handful, he would do the most amusing things all the time. He was short and a bit chubby with a smile that could melt you. His wispy brown hair used to fall into his eyes. He hated having his hair brushed, and I used to have to cut it very quickly before he moved. It was consequently always rather uneven, but he wasn't vain. He had to wear glasses from an early age and looked so endearing in his thick-rimmed blue National Health spectacles. I remember that once he had learned how to dress himself he couldn't stop. He would empty the drawers in his room and put on every item of clothing that he could, giggling all the while. It was often all Artie and George and I could do to undress him again. He looked like a little Michelin man!

Isaac would always share. Whenever there was a toy, he would give it to me, or to one of the boys, and he would always try to feed us food at meal times. I was so sad that Gee-O didn't see all this. I'm sure he loved Isaac in his own way.

I was very proud of George and his intellect, and Artie and his strength.

When Isaac died though, my world collapsed. I had always had a fairly even mood, even when things were going wrong, but losing Isaac floored me, and I hit depths of despair I didn't know were possible. The one glimmer in that black time was when Gee-O turned up at my door shortly after Isaac's funeral. It was as if he knew I now really did need him. It seemed he was ready now and that he could cope much better. He looked after me and did all the practical things that I hadn't the energy or drive to do. He washed me, shopped, and cooked and cleaned for me. Each morning, he would get me up, coax me to take what little breakfast I could manage, and then set about the daily chores. I remember just watching him. Somehow, he had discovered a purpose. He took me to the doctors and got the medication they prescribed for me. I felt empty and hopeless, except for a tiny glimmer that was Gee-O. I realised then that he did love me in his own way and being needed totally for the first time seemed to relax and calm his usually jangled nerves. He had always been a proud man, and I know he hated being on bad terms with his sons. It seemed that Artie was thawing a bit, but I could sense that George was still hot with anger.

I began to respond to the medication and the care. I'm not really sure which did the trick, probably a combination of both, and after a few weeks I was able to see a bereavement counselor about Isaac. She tried to help me feel better about myself, and we talked through what had happened. This helped, although it was very painful at times. I learned to cope with the pain and face it full on. I began to remember the good things about Isaac and to make sense of his short life on Earth. Artie believed everything happened for a purpose, and I had to make sense of things that way.

Gee-O told me that he hated being called that. I was amazed, but so glad that he finally had the courage to speak to me about things. His middle name was William, and so we decided that I would call him Bill. It was sort of like a new beginning. He wanted Gee-O to be forgotten, and most of all he wanted to reconnect with his sons. That was going to take time and patience.

"I know," he said.

For the first time in a long time, I had hope.

*

George
1979

Things did not go so well for Artie.

He managed to get a job in a pub and met a lovely girl with whom he soon struck up a relationship. In no time, Gaby was pregnant with their first child. They married quickly in a Registry office and settled down to wait for the new arrival. Sadly, at 12 weeks the fetus died, and Gaby suffered a miscarriage. Artie spent three sleepless nights visiting Gaby on the gynecology ward at the local hospital. His sleeplessness took its toll. I had a phone call from Gaby at 4 a.m. one morning.

"George, I think Artie's been taking drugs! He's talking rubbish, and I can't get through to him! He's talking 19 to the dozen; I don't know if I should call the police or an ambulance. He just won't sit down."

I went straight round, knowing exactly what had happened. Poor Artie had relapsed again into a manic episode. The stress of losing his baby and the lack of sleep all precipitated a spiral into mania.

When I arrived, Artie was indeed agitated and irritable, but he had some inkling of what was happening.

"Look, Artie, you know you're having a slight relapse. Come with me to the psychiatric emergency clinic, and we can get you some olanzapine. It's a new drug, and good, and won't give you those awful side effects. If we go now, we can be home by tomorrow, I'm sure."

Amazingly, Artie acceded to my request, and I managed to get him into the front seat of my car. He was now mute. I quickly phoned ahead and managed to speak to a duty psychiatrist who was a colleague of one of my doctor friends. She was extremely sympathetic and helpful and agreed to see Artie the moment I could get him there.

We arrived, and I half walked, half carried Artie to the emergency office.

"I'm Dr. Cooper, would it be alright if I talked to you Artie?"

Artie nodded imperceptibly.

"Could you stay and maybe help Artie talk to me?" Dr. Cooper addressed me, and I agreed immediately, very perceptibly. The doctor was kind, thorough, and sensible. Artie nodded occasionally, and I filled in the gaps of the history. We ascertained that Artie's thoughts were racing, but he wasn't hallucinating.

"Look, I don't want to interfere or tell you how to do your job or anything, but do you think... Would it be possible to try..." I mumbled.

"Olanzapine? Yes, I think it would be a good idea in the light of Artie's previous history and his presentation. Artie, would you take a tablet for me?"

Artie nodded, and we were able to get Artie to an observation ward and give him medication.

"You will need to sit with him. I'll be back when I can. If he does not respond, we may need to admit or section him, but let's give this a go."

"Thank you so much; I'm very grateful."

"Not everyone in his position is lucky enough to have an advocate who is also knowledgeable and medical, I can see by the way you interact that he trusts you, even in his manic state. That is good."

We sat for some hours, and Artie fell asleep after taking the medication.

"Let's pop him in a bed," Dr. Cooper said when she reappeared. The nurses helped Artie to a put-up bed in a small room.

Artie slept soundly, and I watched him like a hawk. After 3 hours, he stirred, and I gently prodded him.

"How are you, mate?"

"Head banging, but my mind has slowed down. It was lovely though, and I didn't really want it to stop. But I knew it must."

"Can you control it?"

"Just about, I feel a bit numb but that weird euphoria has gone. Do you think we can go home? Gaby must be sick with worry, and she's lost the baby."

And with that Artie dissolved into tears and great heaves and sobs. I held him until it passed. His emotions were intensely labile.

There was a knock, and Dr. Cooper appeared again.

"Do you want to stay here a while, Artie? We could find a bed, a proper bed for you?"

"If George takes me, could I go home? My wife has just had a miscarriage, and I need to be with her."

"I'll give him the olanzapine and make sure he actually takes it," I added.

"How about you come back and see me tomorrow? I'll be here from 5 p.m."

"It's a deal," I said. "I'll make sure he's here."

And we saw Dr. Cooper every evening for four days. The medication reduced slowly, and Artie was kept on a maintenance dose. He was subdued but not crazy anymore, and he busied himself at home looking after poor Gaby.

For my part, I realised that I needed to see Dr. Cooper. She had been brilliant with Artie, and I felt an amazing bond. I needed to know if this was a passing phase of gratitude or something deeper.

I let a few days pass then headed off to the emergency clinic.

I realised that my heart was beating quickly, and my palms were a bit sweaty. I asked at the desk if I could see Dr. Cooper.

"It's a personal matter," I said to the rather officious receptionist with red hair. "I'm very sorry, Dr. Galley, but Dr. Cooper has gone off duty. I'm afraid I can't give you any more details."

More disappointed than I could have realised, I left the desk and started walking to the exit.

"Hello there, how's Artie doing?"

A familiar voice and that lovely face, Dr. Cooper was clearly just about to walk out, too.

"He's fine. Look, it's you I've come to see."

"Oh, Dear! Are you having some delusions?" She smiled

"Only the ones where you agree to have a drink with me…?"

She laughed, a glorious deep chuckle.

"Look, I am in a rush right now, but how about I give you my number, and we could catch that drink another time?"

I couldn't believe it.

"Yes, that would be great!"

And thus began my courtship with an older woman, who also happened to be a psychiatrist. We started seeing each other regularly. We would go to the cinema, take long walks by the river, and meet for coffee whenever we could and/or when our rosters allowed. Ursula came from a long line of doctors and had devoted herself to medicine. She hadn't really had much time to "date," so we took it very slowly. But I was sure, and I think she was, too, after a few months, that this was relationship that could last.

We were able to talk to one another about anything and often seemed to anticipate what the other was thinking or feeling. It was uncanny. Our age difference didn't seem to matter; I had been through a lot even though I was seven years younger, and my life experiences seemed to enable me to be more mature than a wet behind the ears first-year doctor.

I was concerned that my seeing Ursula would compromise her treatment of Artie, but she was in a good team and passed his everyday care to one of her colleagues.

"I'll keep an eye from afar," she assured me.

The time soon came when I wanted to introduce Ursula to my parents. Ursula was well aware of our family history, having gone into it in depth when she first met Artie, so I thought she would be fine. I persuaded my mother to invite us for a Sunday roast. My father was still at the cottage, and things seemed fairly good.

The big day arrived, and I picked Ursula up from her flat and drove the 10 miles to Mother's cottage.

There was an inviting smell of roast dinner as the front door opened.

"Mother, this is Ursula," I said.

"Do come in, dear," my mother replied, and we went through into the little parlour where my father sat.

"Father, this is Ursula," I moved closer into the room while Ursula waited by the door.

"Good God, boy, what do you think you're doing! That woman's as black as the Ace of Spades," he hissed under his breath. I was shattered and stunned.

I turned on my heel and half dragged, half pulled Ursula out of the house.

"It's alright George, he's just surprised; let's go back in and…"

"He's a monster," I yelled. "Nearly killed my mother and never looked after any of us, best we don't associate with him."

"Look, calm down, I'm not offended, don't forget, I've lived with this sort of thing all my life, it's just fear of the unknown."

"I'm not sure. I just can't trust him."

"But what about your mother? I'd really like to get to know her better."

I was boiling over and couldn't think. Something in me exploded and couldn't be contained.

"Look, maybe this was a bad idea. I'd forgotten what prejudice was like, but I should have known after everything that happened with Isaac over the years."

"George?"

"I'm sorry," I blurted. "I think we should cool it. I need time to process."

"Process? Well, okay, if that's what you want."

And before I could gather my thoughts, Ursula walked off towards the train station.

I was in a daze, I couldn't think straight. The thought of facing years of stress with the woman that I had fallen in love with was clouding my judgment. After years of protecting Mother and Isaac and Artie, I somehow seemed to lack the strength to protect my relationship with Ursula.

I went back to the front door where Mother was standing, looking anxious.

"Oh, George love, your father didn't mean it. He was just, just…"

"Colour prejudiced?" I seethed

"No, dear, it's just that wasn't expecting your friend…"

"Girlfriend."

"Girlfriend to be a black woman. I think he still remembers the looks we got when Isaac was young, and the tittle tattle of neighbours, you know?"

"No, I don't mother, and I don't know why you're protecting him. Look, I'd better go. Sorry about lunch. I'll call you."

"George…"

But I had walked away and gone back to my car. I sat with my head in my hands. Then I drove straight to the football club I had joined, where the lads were having an afternoon kick about. I joined in, still wearing my Sunday best.

"Oi, George mate, cool it, bro!"

My tackles were ferocious and untimed. After 30 minutes of haring around like an idiot, I collapsed exhausted in the dressing room. My trousers were mud splattered and my shins blue. I held my head in my hands again.

"George, come on. Let's have a pint, and you can tell me what's got up your nose! Haven't seen you play that well since you joined the club!"

I managed a weak grin and went off to the bar with the lads.

I don't remember too much about what happened after that, but the team got me home and into bed somehow. When I woke up it was 8 a.m., and I had rounds at 8:30. I was badly hung over and looked appalling. I dragged myself to the shower and threw on some clean clothes.

I couldn't believe my father. In one simple moment, he had ruined my life – again.

10

Ursula, July 1980

I should have known it would not last. A white, working-class boy made good and a black Nigerian woman. I had changed my name from Chukwu to Cooper to fit in better. My life had always been so controlled. It had to be that way. The only chance I could make a success of medicine was for me to be the best of the best. I made myself study, when everyone else was out partying and pairing up. At the age of 37, I had fallen for a white man. It did not make sense. Why had I not ignored those rugged good looks, thick, curly blond hair, and strangely coloured eyes?

George was like no one I had ever met before. Tall and slim, very typically English, but with a humility about him that so many arrogant white men did not possess. And me, a black woman – I should have been attracted to "my own kind," should I not?

None of the men I had been introduced to ever moved me like George. He was so caring about his brother. He seemed haunted somehow. Perhaps it was the ghost of his youngest brother with Down syndrome who had died. He was so compliant and non-confrontational. I had been ready to spend the rest of my life with him, even though he was so young. He had a maturity that was not accounted for by his chronological age, or so I thought.

After the debacle with George's parents, I determined to throw myself into my work. I had been offered a PhD and was procrastinating. I had stupid dreams of marrying and maybe even having a baby, but that biological clock was ticking, and the man I had let my guard slip with had turned out to be like all the rest. I needed to get away and take stock of things while George "processed." I tried not to be hurt and angry and to see it from his perspective, but I had spent my life seeing it from everybody else's perspective and was getting rather tired of that. Before George had come into my life, everything had been ordered, in its place, safe. My role as a psychiatrist had allowed me to be me, in spite of the huge prejudices in the Health Service. Psychiatry was one area where you could be a woman and black and were not noticed for just those things. Not that it was all a bed of roses, and plenty of battles had to be fought. I had been cocooned in my safe haven for too long, and my first adventure outside my comfort zone had ended in chaos. I must have been mad (and I should have known, being a psychiatrist as well!) to contemplate a life outside of my confines.

I decided to take up the PhD and move to a new city.

I had grown up in a caring Christian family with a father who was an ophthalmic surgeon and a mother who was a nurse. I had been nurtured in a church community where my parents worshipped, and I had been made to feel special. My studies had been successful, and I was able to go to the medical school of my parents' choice. I had shown a propensity for psychiatry from my early medical student days, and although I had enjoyed the excitement of acute medicine, psychiatry was a safe option for me. I had learned tolerance, not to show emotion, and to have patience in my chosen discipline: hours of talking it out, seeing every angle, weighing up pros and cons of diagnoses and treatment options for patients.

I immersed myself in my work.

My parents had tried to introduce me to nice Nigerian boys. One particular one stood out; a curate who wanted to sell Jesus to the world. I knew his motives were not humility and goodness, more self-glorification and attention. He was a charismatic man, and I think he would have married me to please his parents, but we both knew there was no future in it. What he required was a mousy lady fawning over his every word. That was not me. In the end, we parted good friends and when we would occasionally meet at a church function, I continued to slap him down if he became too self-absorbed.

Suddenly, I was 37, well-off and stable, but with an inner loneliness that I had to subdue, more and more frequently these days. I had let my guard down and fallen for this boy. A part of my heart still yearned for that idyllic scene, marriage, children, a little house and garden with accepting neighbours and perhaps even a dog. I laughed inwardly.

I had seen too many people with broken dreams, and I decided that the best solution was perhaps not to have dreams at all.

And so, I determined to move on.

I managed to rekindle the PhD offer and was due to set off for Bristol in three weeks.

It was then that I started to look at my calendar.

*

George
July 1980

I should have called Ursula that evening but for some reason I didn't. This was in spite of the fact that I couldn't stop thinking about her. I didn't know why I had been so attracted to her. She was strikingly handsome, I grant you, with deep chocolate brown eyes that looked straight into your heart. She was statuesque and held herself with great poise, but she was also accessible and not haughty. I tried to get the picture of her face out of my mind, but I could not. It did not seem to register that she was from another country, culture, or race.

I had some medical exams coming up soon and really needed to knuckle down. I threw myself into my studies and decided not to see Ursula for a couple of weeks. She had previously sent a good luck card, which I kept on my desk at all times. The day of the first exam arrived, and I took a deep breath and marched into the musty old hall where I would sit the papers.

Luckily, my auto-doc brain took over, and I wrote side after side of paper in answer to the knotty medical conundrums that were placed before me.

Once I had finished the exam I felt a complete catharsis and other thoughts and feelings started to filter back into my consciousness. Mostly they were about Ursula.

When I got home I picked up the phone.

"Can I speak to Dr. Cooper, please?"

I called the psychiatry office.

"Who's calling please?"

"Dr. Galley."

"Oh, I'm sorry, Dr. Galley, but Dr. Cooper doesn't work here anymore. Can I get Dr. Sylvester for you?"

"No, no, thank you. It's fine."

I put the phone down. What had I expected? That Ursula would just sit around waiting for me to become an adult? I had hoped she might, but now, I could see how self-absorbed I had been. My father hadn't put her off; it was me and the years of pent up anger that must have spooked her. How on Earth was I going to learn forgiveness?

First, I had to find Ursula.

The phone rang.

"Thank the Lord!" I cried as I picked it up.

"George, its Gaby. Artie's unwell again. Can you come?"

"Yes, yes, of course. Has he taken any olanzapine? Did you call his key worker?"

"He's calling for you, George."

"Okay; on my way."

*

Artie
July 1980

I didn't want to take the olanzapine any more. It was better than chlorpromazine, but it still numbed my senses. I wanted to cope on my own and help others to learn to do so as well. After my fantastic experiences under Dr. O'-Donnelly, I hadn't really had any faith in other doctors. My GP didn't want to know, other than to give me a repeat prescription, and the only medical person I could trust was George.

Gaby was pregnant for the second time, and I was excited, but terrified. What if she lost the baby again? What if I lost her?

I knew my mind was racing, but it gave me an amazing insight into the universe. When I was high like this, it all came together in an obvious solution. The way the stars shone at night, the way the buses went in threes, there was meaning in everything. I had seen Isaac in a dream, a vision. He was happy and smiling and could speak in many languages. He was showing me the connections of the signs of the zodiac to the colours around me. There was perfect symmetry around him, and he had the answer.

I knew I needed some help, but only from George. George would be able to help me decipher the answer from Isaac, and then I could save the world.

For a long time, I had believed in the afterlife, in spirits that would try to show us the way. It was up to us to make those connections and find meaning. It was so much easier when my mind was racing. Part of me did realize that this was a manic state, but I didn't believe that it was a medical condition. I believed it was part of a plan and could be utilized, if only we knew how. And George and Isaac were the keys.

But it was Mrs. Joy who actually helped me.

I was so restless that night and was dipping in and out of fitful sleep. During one period of half-sleep, I must have dreamed, although it felt like a vision. I was in a beautiful place, golden light shone, waves licked the shores of a white sandy beach, and birds sang melodiously in tall, whispering trees. It felt like paradise. And there was Mrs. Joy, sitting in a deck chair in the middle of the sand. She beckoned me to sit next to her, and I felt an incredible calm come over me. She reached out towards a cradle, and there was Isaac, somehow now a toddler. Isaac waddled over to me and took my hand. Then he was fully-grown and speaking in French, or was it Russian? And then Chinese. Yes, Chinese.

We walked down the beach together, dipping our toes in the warm sea. I could see a dolphin rising and falling with the tide, and at one time, it jumped out of the sea and onto the beach.

"You have a big job ahead of you," said the dolphin, but then it was Mrs. Joy again, smiling so serenely that I felt weightless and free. Then, dark clouds started rolling in off the ocean.

"You can't stop the weather," said Mrs. Joy.

I tried to run back to the beach, but now, I was in a fog, and the light was fading in the top of my vision.

"It'll be alright," whispered the dolphin, and Mrs. Joy, and Isaac, together as if one voice.

When I awoke from this, I felt strangely calmer. My mind wasn't so out of control, but I felt I had work to do, and I needed to write everything down. There was also a part of me that needed to know more about my family. I had been named after poor Uncle Arthur, who had allegedly died in the First World War. I knew little of him, and there seemed to be no one who could tell me more. I decided to write to the War Office and see if I could get some information on his war record. If I knew about my namesake, perhaps I could learn more about myself. There was a part of me that believed we were reincarnated and came back to learn more in another life. Had I been Arthur? Had I died in the First World War?

11
Arthur, 1902-1918

I hate Amelia. She's a pain, and I don't see why I have to do what she tells me. I'm the boy, not her, and she should do what I say. I know how things should work, and girls are silly. I'll show her. I'm going to be a very important person, and then she'll have to look up to me.

"Arthur, come down now. It's tea time," I hear her shriek.

We are in our house in London, and a special tutor comes and teaches me about important things. He taught me Latin and about the Napoleonic wars. My father doesn't want me to go into the army, but I'm going to, and I vow I'm going to be the best soldier who ever fought. Mr. Jamieson said I was very clever and could be a general one day.

I'm going to have to get down out of this tree now; its tea time, and I don't want Amelia eating all the best sandwiches. I put a slug into one of her sandwiches yesterday, and she made such a fuss and told on me. My father cuffed me round the ear, but it wasn't very hard, and it was just for show. I don't really understand why he doesn't want me to go into the army. I guess he's never been one for fights or the like. He's always in his study, painting. Some of the servants say he's a sissy.

The war has started, just like they said it would, and everyone is joining up except my father. He's a coward. I get a lot of jibes from the boys at the academy, but I'll show them. I've got a friend whose brother is in the recruiting office, and he's going to get me papers. I'll keep up the family honour. I told my father and he just looked at me as if I was a stupid boy, but I'll show him.

They've taken me! It's all official, and I go to Colchester tomorrow. They have a camp there, and they say I'll get my uniform, and I'll be in France before I know it. Glory and honour! I can't wait.

My mother doesn't know I've left for Colchester, and I don't think my father will tell her. I'll come home with medals, and then who'll be jealous? Amelia will have to respect me, and I'll be the head of the family.

We're on a boat bound for France now. I'm feeling a bit seasick, but I won't let on. The other lads are fine. I must admit, I'm feeling a bit worried now that it's really happening. They've given me a gun. They think I'm 18. I am quite big, but I can't shave yet. Sarge calls me "Babyface," and I'm a bit annoyed about that. I'll show them.

We've reached the front. It's all mud. Everything is mud, and there are trenches with bodies still covered in mud, dead at their posts. I was sick as soon as I saw them, and the Sarge laughed and said, "Come on, Babyface! Chin up!"

My hands are shaking. We sleep in mud, and I can't get my socks dry. There are patrols every day, and so far, I've just stayed here and been on watch in the trench. It's raining hard again, and nothing ever seems dry. Sarge has just brought me a cup of cocoa, as he said I looked rank. We're going over the top tomorrow. No one's ever comes back when they go over the top. I can sometimes peek over the trench wall, and there's barbed wire and more mud. I haven't seen a German yet. Barnes got hit in the shoulder, and there was blood mixed with the mud. We dragged him along the trench and a medic came. He was screaming so badly.

We're going over the top.

The sound is deafening; I can't see for the smoke and the mist. There's a lot of yelling. My leg feels very hot, and I'm lying down by some barbed wire. There's more yelling and gunfire. They're dragging me along, and it hurts like hell. I think I'm going to black out, but I don't. We're going backwards.

I'm in the dugout and a medic is slicing through my trousers to the wound.

"Get him to the field hospital," yells someone.

I'm on a stretcher, and now, I'm in a tent. There are men everywhere. Some have only one leg, some only one arm. Some look as though their brains have been blown out. There are bloodstained bandages and more mud. I'm in a bed next to a dying soldier.

"Someone get the padre!" I hear.

A nurse brings me some gruel. I gag on it, but some goes down. It is warm and salty.

Hours pass; days pass.

"There's an infection here; need to amputate."

I realize it's me they're talking about. Babyface. What am I doing here?

They tell me to bite down hard, but I'm screaming. The pain is indescribable.

"I want my mother!"

But she doesn't come. The pain gradually dulls, and I fall into a restless stupor. I'm sweating, even though it's freezing.

"Still infected. Nothing more we can do."

I am on a waiting list, a waiting list for death. I don't know what use any of this has been. We were duped. Stories of glory. Rubbish. It's just blood and guts and gore and mud and death. I would even be glad to see Amelia... Just one more time. They say your life flashes by you in an instant just before you are about to die.

A nurse sits by me and holds my hand. I am shaking uncontrollably now. I just want it to stop.

*

George
July 1980

I found Artie sitting at home with the table strewn with drawings and maps and ciphers. He has been up all night, trying to put the reams of paper he had written on into some sort of order.

"George, thank God. You can help me now."

"Yes, of course, I will, but don't you think you should try to get some sleep? We'll never be able to get this straight if we're both exhausted," I said.

"I'm fine."

"But you're not, are you? Not really. Gaby says you haven't eaten or slept for 24 hours."

"I don't want any drugs. Look, I saw it all. I know we need to work hard, but Isaac and Mrs. Joy and the dolphin, they were there. They're going to help."

"Look, if you want to work on this properly, you need some rest. Why don't I give you a half tablet of olanzapine?"

Miraculously, Artie agreed. I could see his inner battle between mania and the much less pleasant cold light of real day. There was a bit of to-ing and fro-ing, but eventually, he took a half tablet with a hot cup of sweet tea that Gaby had made.

(The medicinal benefits of hot sweet tea are not to be underrated!)

We got him to bed, and after an hour or so, he was asleep.

"How are you doing?" I asked Gaby.

"I'm so tired with the pregnancy, and this doesn't help. I know he means well and truly believes in all this stuff," she pointed to the paper-strewn table, "but it is a drain."

We sat for a while and then I let Gaby go off to bed in the spare room.

For the first time in a while, I was able to gather my thoughts. I knew that Artie had manic episodes and probably depressive ones, too, but was medication the answer? Some of the patients I'd seen with similar conditions had been put on lithium, with reasonable effect. The drug needed to be regularly monitored though, too little and it wasn't worth taking, and too much and it was toxic. I wished Ursula were with me to discuss this. I decided that each individual person had to be treated on his or her own merits, and that there wasn't a "one size fits all" answer. The busy NHS often tried to sell that solution, but it wasn't right. My mind grappled with this for a while, blocking out thoughts of Ursula which kept creeping back in.

"Morning, George."

I must have fallen asleep in the armchair.

"Artie, are you okay?"

"Not too bad, George. I think I need to take another half dose of olanzapine tonight, and then maybe a quarter tomorrow night. What do you think?"

"Yes, yes, that's perfect… I can pop in and see how you are each evening."

"That would be great, George, I really appreciate it. I've told Gaby that I'll only spend two hours a day on my 'charts,' as she calls them. I know you don't think they're important, but I think it's worth trying."

"Look, who am I to say what's important or not, what's real or not? I think what's important is that you take control. You know that you can't be in a manic state all the time, and only you can tell how much or how far your treatment needs to go. But, I do think you need some psychological help, talking therapy help.

"Will you call your liaison nurse today?"

"I'll think about it."

"Okay, fair enough."

I left Artie and Gaby a little less heavy of heart and went back to my digs to get ready for work. That phone call to Ursula would have to wait till this evening.

12

Bill (Gee-O), 1980

I made no apology for what I said to George. I wasn't colour prejudice, but I knew what could happen when things don't fit properly. A white man and a black woman, doesn't fit, not in our world.

Maybe one day, maybe in years to come – when I'm dead and buried.

We needed to stick to our own.

George hates me. Hates me for leaving him with Isaac.

Isaac didn't fit in our world either, and it nearly killed Sally. But it wasn't Isaac's fault. He'd have been better off in a home with his own kind much earlier on. Birds of a feather should stick together. I don't understand what's happening to the world. The old order is being blown away.

I don't mean that the Nazis had the answer, trying to exterminate Jews and homosexuals and whatever. But different people need to stay in their own communities. They're happier there. All this integration doesn't work; it just leads to heartache and misunderstanding when it all goes horribly wrong.

I knew. I'd seen it. I'd really seen it.

How was I going to square it with George? I only wanted what was best for him. I never had any role models for parenting. I hardly saw my mother and my father. Amelia was the nearest thing to a parent, but she was dark and troubled, and I sensed I was a nuisance to her. I always struggled to understand what love meant. I realised now that my sons were the most important things in my life, and I really didn't want our relationships to be rotten or nonexistent.

Strangely, Sally was the only one who really understood me. She forgave me, even after I had abandoned her. She understood my mental anguish as though she had experienced anguish of her own. Her depression was horrible. But the drugs helped, and she was now back to her sweet, kind, quiet self. I knew she was torn between George and me, and I knew I had stepped out of line by blurting out in front of the nice black woman. I knew that I was living in a kind of time warp and hadn't moved on, not really moved on from my bleak childhood where I had never felt loved or valued. Sally gave me that back, that chance. I wanted to make it up to her.

She told me to wait and not make things worse with George.

I realised now how much I hurt her and how much I lost in those years when I left. She was an amazing person, and I was lucky to have her

"It'll work its way right," she said to me.

So, I'd wait… For her.

While I waited, I needed to get strong again, mentally strong. I wanted to understand what happened to me in the war and where my anxiety came from. I decided to seek help, to see a shrink. It would cost money I know, but I owed it to Sally to be a better person. I owed it to my sons to be a better person than my father.

I decided I wanted to go to Harley Street and get a top doctor, but I didn't know how to go about it. No one in the small circles that I moved in would have the foggiest idea. I told Sally, as I wanted to be completely open with her, and she suggested I start with the family doctor. I made an appointment and took out my old suit and put on my regimental tie that I had kept locked in a cupboard for years.

When I entered the doctor's office, it was the first thing that he noticed.

"Good day Mr. Galley. I don't think we've met before."

He stood up and shook my hand; a firm, dry grip, which I appreciated. I looked around the room, and it was sparsely furnished. A large desk with some papers on that the doctor sat at, a chair for the patient, and a couch in the corner, presumably where he examined them physically.

"I see you're from the old 5th Winchester Regiment. Jolly good. Now, what can I do for you?"

"I want to get my head straight."

"I see," the doctor mused. He was middle-aged, like myself, with thick-rimmed glasses and greying hair slicked back with oil. He was wearing a smart jacket over a white shirt and plain blue tie. He could have been the conservative candidate for Harrow.

"Well, you'd better tell me all about it." He smiled.

I related the symptoms I had experienced in the war and at times of stress. I told him sketchily about my father and mother, and then about the incident with George. Strangely, I said nothing of Isaac at that first meeting.

"We've had 20 minutes already, Mr. Galley, so I'm afraid you're going to have to make another appointment."

"What I really want is an appointment to see a specialist, please," I said quickly.

"Look, I think I might be able to help you myself, but we're going to need more time. I'm a member of a special group of GPs who like to discuss patients' symptoms and problems and to endeavor to help without the aid of a referral when appropriate. From what you've told me so far, I think we could work together for a bit. It means you putting in some effort, and it won't always be easy, but what do you say?"

I had felt at ease talking with this man, and although he was my age and dressed rather conservatively, I did not feel him to be judgmental or prejudiced in any way. Seeing him would save money, and what did I have to lose?

"Look, I can see you once a week at the end of my Wednesday morning surgery. I can give you about 45 minutes, and we could see how it goes."

I agreed and found myself already looking forward to the next session.

As Wednesday loomed, I tried to think of what it was I wanted to say to the doctor. My mind started to go blank, and I began to panic. What if what I had was going to get worse again, and I let Sally down once more? My palms were sweaty, and my guts were churning.

I pulled myself together enough to get to the doctor's, and I knew as I entered the room he could tell I was distressed.

"Sit down, and tell me what you're feeling," he said

"What I'm feeling, what I'm feeling…" I mumbled. I'd never been good at expressing feelings. "Scared, worried it's all coming back, that I can't get better."

"Well, that's understandable."

"Is it? You mean, you don't think I'm hopeless?"

"Anxiety is a funny old thing, and it takes many guises. It's a mimic and a chameleon. But once you've identified it, it loses its power. After all, you were the one who created it, and you can make it disappear."

I settled down and found myself talking again. Everything poured out and was obviously pretty jumbled. I couldn't picture my mother. There was the shape of a woman with Victorian style dress, but no face. I couldn't recall my mother's face.

"Look, how would you feel if we took this bit by bit? You can choose the bit you want to talk about, for example: your relationship with Sally, or your father, or your sons, and then we can try and sort out where you are with everything and how it relates to your symptoms. Get some order."

"Sounds good."

"Well, time is up today, but I want you to come back next week with a topic and some thoughts and feelings about that segment of your life. Especially feelings."

"I've never been very good at talking about my feelings"

"Well, you've done so already to me without too much trouble. Let's just see what happens, no pressure"

I attended the doctor on Wednesdays, and sometimes, there were tears (I couldn't believe how emotional I'd get), and sometimes, I clammed up and was lost for words. Gradually, I started to feel like a whole person, possibly for the first time in my life. I was able to come to terms with my actions, not necessarily excuse them, but definitely understand them. I felt a calmness and tranquility that had eluded me for so long, and my symptoms, when they occasionally did appear, were given little credence and so never overtook me. My relationship with Sally grew in strength, and I moved back into the main bedroom. We felt like a family again. I just needed to improve my relationship with my sons, including Isaac.

One day, I went to the crematorium and knelt by the plaque in the garden of rest that marked his ashes. Inwardly, I spoke to him and asked him to forgive me for running away. I wanted a sign, something to let me know he'd heard, but that was to come later.

I still couldn't picture my mother.

13
Mary, 1922

I have no choice but to leave Charles in London. Amelia is perfectly capable of looking after him, and now, she can have a baby to look after too. I can't bear to look at him or have him near me. How I ever gave him children, I know not. Losing Arthur was dreadful, but once I knew what Charles was like, I couldn't bear the children either.

What a mess this has all turned out to be! Only the Major was any sort of solace. I knew he wouldn't leave his silly wife, goodness only knows why. I didn't want to be pregnant.

In the end, I didn't tell the Major.

It was all too complicated, and my sisters were forever fussing around me like a prize bee. I lied. I said it was Charles' baby. They couldn't understand why I wasn't with Charles. I couldn't tell them. So, I spent as much time as I could with the Major. Love? Oh, I'm not sure what it was. He was attractive and dashing and powerful. I asked him to manage some of my finances, and he invested the money in his plantations in South Carolina. He always paid good dividends to me, and I asked no questions. And, besides, it was a good excuse to see him. We'd have dinner. It would be so easy. He and I would talk for hours. Then we would conduct our little ruse.

My sisters were so stupid. They never guessed, and the lieutenant was so helpful. He knew, of course. I think he had a fancy for Amelia, but he was married. She clearly fell for him. Well, it would do her good to know how painful love is. She was weak, of course, like her father.

I would languish in the Major's strong arms, and he would show me what a true man was.

No, not love. Something close perhaps, I must admit.

I was quite put out when he told me he couldn't visit as often and that his office in New York was closing down. I didn't complain. I had money and servants and friends aplenty in Sussex.

The pregnancy was terrible. I was so ill and had to take to my bed. They said it was dangerous at my age and that sometimes babies would be deformed or something. My sisters were useless. What did they know of pregnancy? It was truly awful. I couldn't wait to be rid of the child. I needed to get my figure back, and I hated being so bloated. They took it away, thank goodness, and Amelia and the wet nurse took over. Good riddance. I didn't want the child, but I wasn't going to jeopardize my health with any malpractice. I thought about it, getting rid of it, but I couldn't bear the idea.

So, I pretended it was Charles' and got on with it. It was such a nuisance. It had been nearly a year, and thank goodness, I didn't have to see the boy. I wanted to forget.

But now, I was bored. The lieutenant was visiting to clear up some of the major's business, and I have invited him over for dinner. I didn't tell Amelia.

Anyway, she was too busy with the baby to have time for anything else. I had to admit, I was curious about the plantations. And the lieutenant was a wonderful gossip, and very attractive, too. We were to have a very jolly evening.

"Lankhurst, I need you now. I want the green dress this evening, brings out the colour of my eyes. Hurry! What on Earth have you been up to? I've been waiting hours!"

I heard the bell go, and I presumed the lieutenant was shown into the drawing room. It was a good size and well furnished. I told the cook to do the pheasant that Farmer Goode had delivered that morning. I knew the lieutenant liked game.

I checked my appearance and rose slowly to descend the stairs. Lankhurst hadn't fastened my gown properly, and I scolded her appropriately. You just couldn't get good servants anymore. They were sloppy and useless.

I greeted the lieutenant, and my sisters entered the room. I scowled at them, and they sat in the corner and took out their books. The butler came across to me with my whisky and offered the lieutenant a drink.

"Whatever the good lady is having," he smiled.

"Well, now, I want you to tell me all about the major and his plantations. Its two weeks since he left; you must have finished up all the loose ends by now?"

"Oh, yes, Ma'am. The major sends his very best regards. He's mighty sorry not to be here himself, but I'm sure I can fill you in on anything you might want to know. He told me to look after you and your every need."

"You are too kind. And of course, you will stay the night. I have instructed Lankhurst to make up the red room for you."

"How kind!"

"And how is your wife?"

"She's fine, Ma'am. Much taken with our new young son, Emery. He's number four. I was mighty glad to be sent here on behalf of the major though. I'm no good fussing around the nursery!"

"No, indeed! Not really a soldier's place."

The lieutenant smiled, his flashing white teeth gleaming in the firelight.

"Ma'am, you look a little chilled. Can I stoke up the fire for you?"

"Well, how thoughtful! The servants are so lax; you don't know how it vexes me. They need a good talking to."

"Ah, now that's something the major would never tolerate. His servants jump to attention at the very mention of his name, and so it should be. Now, is that better?"

The fire roared, and I could feel the colour rising in my cheeks.

"Oh, yes, much better!"

Lankhurst appeared and announced dinner was served.

We sat convivially, and the lieutenant devoured his meal. I must say, I liked a man who ate heartily. Charles only picked at his food, but the major would tear into a steak with relish! I managed a little mouthful or two of the pheasant. Cook hadn't done it properly, although the lieutenant didn't seem to mind.

My sisters retired to their rooms, and the lieutenant and I were left having a nice little brandy.

"Now, tell me, what happens on these plantations? Are they making a profit still?"

"Well, there's folks that would have them Negroes freed up. Now the major is rebelling against such stupidity, and he's making them Negroes pay by working them harder."

"Good, he's so masterful. I like that."

"Yes, Ma'am. He's a terror all right! But cotton production is holding, and we're hoping for a good season."

"I'm glad to hear it."

"But it needs more investment. The major wanted me to tell you that your money is safe, but it's not going to get repaid anytime soon."

"As long as I have my dividends."

"Oh, yes, Ma'am – no question."

My glass was empty, and the lieutenant got up to fill it.

"Oh, where are those servants! I'm so sorry you are inconvenienced."

"Not at all, Ma'am, my pleasure. It has always been a pleasure to serve such a beautiful lady as yourself. Elegance and poise, now that's what I look for in a lady. Elegance and poise, and you do have those things in Spades!"

He was flirting unashamedly now. I was flattered and wondered how far he would take it. I was bored and needed distraction, and here it was. I cast my mind back to when he'd asked to take Amelia out for tea. Something had happened. I wasn't completely blind, although I did not care to hear the gory details. I couldn't help wondering if he'd had the audacity. Looking at him attending to my every whim, I rather fancied he probably did! I decided to tease him.

"Your wife must be such a forgiving lady, allowing you out of her sight to attend the major. Doesn't she worry you'll stray?"

"My now, Ma'am, whatever could you mean?"

He laughed, and his eyes twinkled.

After an hour or so, and after stories of the plantation and the laziness of the Negroes and problems for the poor Major, it was time to retire.

"Lankhurst will show you to your room. It's been a pleasure, Lieutenant."

"The pleasure was all mine. And may I ask where your room is, just in case of any intruders in the night?"

"My, do you think we are at risk of attack?"

"Well, you can never be too careful."

"My room is the first on the right at the top of the stairs"

"Thank you, Ma'am. I will make sure no harm befalls you in the night."

Lankhurst appeared at the summons of the bell and led the lieutenant upstairs. Afterward, she attended to me, and I pulled back the crisp, white sheets of the four-poster bed and slowly raised my legs. I wasn't old, not yet. I'd had such traumas, but I was sure my body and my beauty were still sufficient for a man like the lieutenant.

I didn't have to wait long for the gentle knock at the door.

14

Ursula, August 1980

It had been three weeks. I was going to visit my GP that evening. I had not been feeling very well, and I had to visit the toilet a lot. I did not know if I had an infection, or maybe even diabetes. I could not rationalize my symptoms. Being a doctor did not help. I kept thinking of the worst possible diagnosis.

I booked an appointment and left my office in Bristol early to make sure I was on time. The waiting room was heaving, and I really need not have bothered. It was over an hour later that I was finally called in to see the GP

"How can I help?"

"Thank you. I am a bit worried about frequency of micturition."

"Ah, you're a doctor I take it! What field do you work in?"

"I am a psychiatrist."

"Gosh, well done, you! It must be a very stressful area to work in. Are you at the local unit?"

"No, I am actually doing a PhD at the moment."

"Wonderful, wonderful! Now tell me a little more about yourself."

"Well, I have just moved to Bristol in the last three weeks, and since then I have been peeing more than usual. There is no burning or stinging though. I am hungry, but sometimes, I just cannot face food."

"I see… Anything else?"

"Well, I suppose I may be a bit stressed. We all are, I know. I did have a relationship break up, well, sort of breakup, I think. Well, I have not heard from him, although, he does not actually know where I am. I am babbling, sorry…"

"No, no, carry on."

"And, oh Lord… I have not seen my period this month."

"Ah, when was the last one, can you remember?"

"No, no – I cannot. Oh, goodness!"

"Look, don't worry. I think its best if we test your urine for infection, diabetes, and…"

"Pregnancy," I murmured.

"Yes, precisely. Would that be alright?"

"Yes, do you…"

"Pop out with this bottle, and come straight back in. I'll make a few notes while you're gone."

"Yes, thanks, of course."

I returned with the evidence, the little tube that could determine the rest of my life.

"Sit down over here, and I'll check. Right, that's easy- no sugar or protein. How would you feel if this pregnancy test was positive?"

"I do not know. I had not thought… Well, yes, I had, I mean, I do want children. I am 37, and I know it is not good after 37."

"Well, it's positive. It's probably a bit of a shock. It might help you to take some time to think about things. Is there anyone you can talk to? Can you tell your partner, do you think?"

"Yes, I will have to."

"You're right, of course. The risks in pregnancy are a bit higher when you're in your later thirties. Is there anything in particular you might be worried about?"

"My, er, boyfriend, his brother suffered from Down syndrome."

"Yes, Down's is more of a risk for you. We can do scans and blood tests and, of course, amniocentesis if you want. But these are all things to think about later. Right now, you need a bit of time to process and talk. How about if we meet up in a couple of days?"

"Yes, yes, of course."

"Look, shall I make you an appointment – say Friday, 4:30 p.m.?"

"Yes, thank you."

I left with a little appointment slip in my hand. I was in a daze. Pregnant, that was a bittersweet pill to swallow.

Artie
August 1980

A letter arrived from the War office. It was Uncle Arthur's war record.

There wasn't much of it.

Galley, Arthur Percival. DOB 1/3/1899

I knew for a fact that this was wrong. He must have lied about his age.

Action: the Somme 1917. Wounded.

Treated at field hospital. No further record.

Could he have survived? It seemed incredible, but maybe my namesake had not been killed in the war, maybe I wasn't his reincarnation. It seemed I would never know, and I needed to stop my mind galloping off in all directions.

I felt better. I'd connected with my uncle, and although I didn't have any concrete answers, it was something tangible, a part of his life.

I started to look at all the pages of scribbles that I'd made during and after my stay in the mental hospital. I could understand how people might think they were nonsense. I started to read through some of them. The beginning related to my first "breakdown," and I read with some surprise how clear the writing was, in spite of the many spelling mistakes.

When I woke up that morning and did all the usual things to get ready for work, I did not know what was going to happen that day. I was in a state of high emotion. All the news that week had been about IRA and bombings. I prayed to God for peace, like the rest of the country. I had not had proper sleep for weeks, and for the past five nights, I had had no sleep at all.

There was a plan in my head that I was going somewhere that day. In my own mind, I thought everybody knew the plan. It was as if everything had been leading up to this day, this moment, destiny, and fate. My emotions were churning, and as I got to the barracks, I could see all the different colours of the vehicles so vividly. Each one meant something to me, and I waved to each one.

When I started the day in the usual way, drilling, breefings, phisical exercises, I had a special pen in my top pocket. The corporal on watch that day had a black badge on. I knew this was a sign that he was from "the dark side." That was alright, though, as everything had to be balanced, good and evil alike.

I kept thinking that once all the squaddies were assembled in the dormitory (we were spending a week on maneuvers), the pattern would be complete. It was as if everyone was following a sequence of events, but I was the only one who knew what was going on.

It all seemed like a big pattern, and everything that happened fell into place and made sense to me.

By the time we were all assembled in the dorm, I had become so high that I must have been hallucinating. What followed was one of the most extraordinary events of my life. The squaddies didn't know what to make of me, and by this time, I had taken all my clothes off and was singing.

I tried to tell one of them what it all meant, especially things like it didn't matter what colour you were and that I was trying to identify who God was. It must have been such a jumble, and one of the squaddies thought I was possessed. He went and got his Bible, so I just went along with it and continued singing and chanting.

It was then that George arrived. I think I must have been pretty much out of control at this point, and I knew he was upset. I seemed to have incredible phisical strength and felt all-powerful. I remember that George managed to carm things a bit.

I remember thinking so much about Isaac. About his childlike ways and his love of Father Christmas. I remembered that he was always talking about Christmas, and as the holidays approached, we tried to think of ways for him to join in with the Christmas fun. For a while, Isaac had attended a day centre and there had always been a Christmas party and a Father Christmas to visit the children with a sack of toys. Someone in the counsel had decided that this was a waste of money and that the "handicapped kids" didn't know or understand about Christmas so it wouldn't matter if the party and presents were cut. I had tried to complain, but no one was really interested.

Once George arrived, he tried to slow my mood down with soothing words that made sense to me. I had to be taken to a hospital. I remember trying to explain to a man with a wispy beard what I was going through. I remember being given an injection, and the doctor saying, "He should be knocked right out with this medication."

They didn't realize I could hear every word that was said and that it was even magnified in my brain.

I ended up in a loony ward where I was to spend the worst seven days and nights of my life.

During the day, everyone just sat there. Some were smoking; some were moaning. I sat there, too, trying to work out how to both help all these poor souls and also get them all out of there.

The nights were the worst. Sleep was impossible. People were crying, causing disturbances, even trying to climb into my bed.

The ward that I was on was called Barbara Ward and everyone, whatever their problem, was just thrown in there together. There were males and females and only a few nurses to cope with everybody and everything. It was so stressful at times that I was surprised the nurses weren't admitted themselves!

The ward was quite large and Victorian, and everything was grey. The floors, the walls, the white basins, and toilets were all actually grey. There was an area for eating, a sitting room, and a TV area. Everywhere was covered in a cloud of cigarette smoke. This was in spite of no smoking signs, which no one took any notice of. A general background noise of coffing and spluttering accompanied everything that went on in that God forsaken place.

The drugs were awful. They dulled some of my body and brain but not my senses, and I felt aware and clear in myself. I felt that nothing had changed since the dark ages, and that if this was a hospital, how was anyone ever going to get better? I still didn't apply this to myself, as I thought that there was nothing mentally wrong with me, and I was just an onlooker.

The first night was horrendous. I was put in a bed right next to the bathroom. There were lights on everywhere and nurses checking on patients throughout the night. There was a huge mixture of people and a whole range of problems, young and old, male and female, chronic disorders to acute breakdowns and mostly lots of depression. Depression and smoke filled the air and every little nook and cranny. I began to see the other inmates, and as I fashioned characters around them, I started to think of actors who could play their parts in a wonderful film, which would expose all this for what it was. A nightmare.

Two patients stood out for me, both resembling famous actors. I called them by the actors' names and often wondered what was going on inside their heads. I never found out. There was Bob Hope, who looked as though he had never experienced hope in his troubled life, and Greta Garbo. She was as enigmatic as her actress counterpart and sat in a corner, clearly "wanting to be alone."

It seemed to me that a lot of these patients were never going to get the real help they needed, and so I started on a crusade in my mind, both for these patients and for Isaac and people like him. The world needed to know that the way society dealt with them, with us, with me, was just wrong.

The drugs that they gave me made my heart race and my head pound. All I wanted was sleep, but just as I started to drift off, a bright light was shone in my eyes as the night staff did their 4 a.m. check.

Eventually, the first night ended, and patients started getting up, some bustling around. One old boy shuffled off to what seemed to be a kitchen area, so I followed him. There was coffee and tea and a kettle, so I made myself a cup and sat at a table. I felt so dirty in the gown that had been put on me and all I wanted was a shower. I felt sure that once they saw me shaved and clean they would know they had made a mistake in making me stay here.

On a chair nearby, there was a lady who had been in the bed opposite me on the ward. She had got up and got dressed in the middle of the night and disappeared. I remember thinking at the time, I wonder where she is going?

I noticed that she had two carrier bags stuffed full. She was the ward bag lady. I think she just came and went as she pleased and nobody took any notice of her.

After a coffee, I felt a bit better, and the ward continued to lurch into life (of sorts).

I could not find anyone who would let me have a shower, and I was told to find someone with keys. Why on Earth would a bathroom be locked? I thought. There were a couple of basic basins and two toilets, so I washed as best I could with the cold, hard soap on the stand. I remember thinking that there was no dignity in this place at all.

My mind started to wake up a little, and I tried to remember the events of the previous day. I kept thinking that this was all a big joke and a celebrity would soon walk in and say, "Fooled you!"

I wanted to see a doctor and explain this had all been a big misunderstanding. There seemed to be a vague routine to the ward, so I watched, took it all in, and went along with it. I realised I was in a line waiting for medication. I didn't want anything. I hated any sort of drug, and I only took paracetamol in a dire emergency. Someone called my name, and I felt very apprehensive.

"Tablets or liquid?" Was shouted at me.

I had hidden some of the tablets that had been given me earlier, pretending meekly to have swallowed them.

I opted for liquid, as that was what you gave children, so I guessed it would be much milder. Good God, was I wrong.

The effect of the drug was horrendous and quite fast. My pulse started to race, my heart pounded, and my head felt as if it were in a vice. My vision blurred, and then I was seeing double with a deafening buzzing in my ears. I felt as though this was worse than death. The medication made me drowsy, but I wanted to sleep in the night, not daytime. No one had spoken to me or explained what the medicine was for or was going to do to me.

Then, miracles of miracles, George appeared. I managed to persuade him that I was well enough to go home, and he went off to get my discharge papers. I went back to my bed and started putting a few things in a carrier bag that was there. Then I made my way to the door and tried to open it. It was locked. I shook the handle couple of times.

The next thing I knew, two burly nurses pinned me down and wispy beard was jabbing me. The injection on top of the previous drugs knocked me out completely.

*

I couldn't remember writing about my experiences in such detail at the time, and was struck by the rambling, misspelt words. Reading the journal that I had written so soon after the events brought it all crashing back to me and I started to panic.

I swore to myself that I had to learn from my experiences and keep my mind functioning in reality. Gaby was depending on me, and we were embarking on another of those roller-coaster rides through pregnancy. Every day would be a challenge, for both of us. I knew I had to keep my mind occupied and my sleep pattern regular. If my mind started racing too much, I could end up in a psychiatric ward again, and I couldn't let that happen.

A job.

I knew some men who were working on a building site and had met a couple of them in the local pub. I knew I had to cut down on my visits to that particular place, but this was a time when I really needed to see some friendly faces.

I told Gaby I was going out for a short time and ran off down the road to the Red Arms. Inside, it was warm and inviting, and as expected, two or three of the lads from the site were there.

"Artie, mate, come and have a beer!"

A couple of pints later, we were all chatting freely.

"Look fellas, do you think there might be a job for me down on the site? I can do anything. I'm pretty strong."

"Best ask Smelly the foreman," one chap said.

"Smelly?" I asked.

"Mr. Smellington, bit of a git, but I know for a fact they're not meeting the deadlines, and I reckon he might be worth a try for a job, probably only temporary though."

"Yeah, with that baby coming, Artie, it's worth a go. I'll back you up. Meet me tomorrow at 7 a.m. sharp down on the site, and we'll see what we can do."

"Thanks so much, lads! That's great!"

With a heart much lighter and a master plan for the future, I trotted back home. Already my mind had raced ahead – I'd done really well on the site, the boss had spotted me and made me a foreman on another job. I finished it in record time, got promoted to director of the company…

"Whoa," I scolded myself. "One step at a time."

The next morning, I was up at six, made a coffee, and kissed a sleepy Gaby goodbye. As he had promised, the lad from the site was there to meet me, and we went to the office to wait for Mr. Smellington. He finally arrived, a rather small weasel like man with ideas far, far above his "foreman" station. The lad spoke first and buttered "Smelly" up very nicely, saying what a good job he was doing, what great pressure he must be under. He then introduced me as a "superhero of a worker."

"What's yer name?"

"Arthur Galley, sir."

"Experience?"

"Well, er, I've been in the army, lots of hard tough work there…"

"Why d'yer leave?"

"Er, personal reasons. Wife's pregnant, sir, and I need something soon."

"Hmmm , and you think he's alright, do you, Jenkins?"

"Yes, Mr. Smellington, good as gold."

"Well, I suppose we could do with a bit of extra muscle. That wimp Jones has gone off sick again, probably have to get rid of him. Give you a week's trial."

"Thank you, sir, thank you!"

"Right, Jenkins, take him over to the hut and get him togged up; we're shifting some of the windows today. Damned heavy, so mind he's strong enough! Jenkins, I'm relying on you."

We walked off towards the site stores, and I nudged Jenkins.

"I owe you one."

"You sure do, Artie!" He grinned.

It all seemed to go well that day and the next. I went home to Gaby and told her I'd found a job and that everything was going to be fine. She was now 15 weeks pregnant, and the sickness was wearing off. The hospital was checking her regularly, and I remember she'd been asked if she wanted to find out about the baby's "chromosomes," although we weren't quite sure what that meant. We'd both decided against anything that could harm the baby, now that the little one inside her was starting to grow more and more, and neither Gaby nor I wanted any needles or anything like that. I was slowly winning my internal battle and found myself consciously slowing my thoughts. There was still so much going on in my brain, but I tried to focus on one thing at a time and get through each day.

At the end of the week, Smelly asked for volunteers over the weekend to shift more glass. Jenkins declined, but I said I'd be happy to help out. Time and a half for the Sunday was too good to turn down.

Come Sunday, I wasn't feeling great, may have been starting a cold or something, but I got up at six and made my way into the yard. The weather was turning, and a cold breeze was blowing from the north. My fingers were raw.

The chap called Jones came over and asked me to help him pick up a large sheet of pane glass. Jones – he obviously wasn't well, snorting and sneezing everywhere, but had struggled into work for fear of losing his job.

We had to walk along a rather narrow raised walkway with a huge piece of glass. Jones was wobbling around, and then suddenly there was a great gust of wind. Jones simply let go and I was left tottering with this damn great pane of glass, trying to keep it upright. I stumbled, and my legs buckled. The glass fell and shattered on top of me with a large shard sticking itself right into my arm.

"Quick, get the gaffer," yelled Jones to some of the other lads and raced off towards the office. The men came over and started picking glass off me, bit by bit.

"You hurt mate? Saw what happened, that tosser Jones."

Smelly rushed up.

"Christ alive, call an ambulance! He's bleeding like a stuck pig!"

The large cut to my left arm was oozing red sticky blood. Somehow, I pulled the huge piece of glass out of my rather numb arm.

"Shouldn't have done that, mate!" cried one bloke as blood shot everywhere; another had found the first aid bag and managed to produce some wadding which he shoved on my wound.

"Press hard," said Smelly.

Ten minutes later, an ambulance had arrived, and I was being carted off to the local casualty department.

"Don't want him back again," muttered Smelly under his breath.

"But it was Jones' fault!" I yelled. "Just ask him!"

But Jones was nowhere to be seen.

15

George, September 1980

I got a call from a casualty sister informing me that my brother had been in an accident. My mind leapt from one scenario to another as I jumped into my little 2 CV 6 and sped (well, top speed for that car was about 40 mph!) to the hospital.

When I arrived, Artie was just coming out of theatre. He'd been stitched back together by one of the top orthopedic surgeons, who evidently was always on the lookout for the type of injury that Artie had sustained. Not for the first time in his life, a top doctor had singled out Artie and put him back on track.

As he came 'round, I sat by his bedside and read one of the magazines on the side table. It was a relatively new copy of the British Medical Journal, so I busied myself looking at the latest research and then flipped to the back pages where the adverts were. For some reason, something caught my eye, and I found myself reading about a unique opportunity in Western Australia. There was a call for a young doctor to be a medic in a new mining company just outside Perth (I was later to learn that "just outside" meant over 500 miles or more!). I knew from the article that they were also recruiting labourers to work in the mines. It didn't register then, but over the next few days an idea began to foment in my mind.

I chatted to Artie, who was pretty down, and told him I was working on something for the both of us.

When Artie was discharged a few days later, his wounds were more or less healed, and he was told to have a course of physiotherapy to finalize his treatment. Gaby was stressed and had asked one of her distant cousins to come and stay for a bit, more moral support than anything. The cousin had been in contact and wanted to come immediately. Strangely, this cousin was called Joy, and I immediately thought of Mrs. Joy from my childhood. Joy turned out to be just that and helped Gaby pick herself up by being a silent but effective housekeeper. She asked for nothing in return and just said "she was glad of the company."

When Artie arrived home, he was fairly quiet, very unlike him, and I began to fear he might be dipping into a depressive state. This would fit with his manic episodes and make the diagnosis of a bipolar disorder a truly terrifying likelihood.

I had to do something.

One week later, I visited their little house and took Artie outside for a walk.

"Look, I've got an idea that might help both of us. There's a job going for me in Australia, and I've already made inquiries. I've got an interview next week. I know they're looking for good workers and the pay is phenomenal."

"What about Ursula?"

"Haven't seen her for a few weeks. I suspect it's over, so this would be a good way to forget and move on. The beauty is that the workers can do one month on and one month off so you'd be able to come back in a few months with a pocket full of cash and I could send you home each month to be with Gaby. Joy is doing a grand job, and I know she wants to stay for a bit."

"What about Gaby? Won't she be upset?"

"Maybe at first, but if she knows we're together, I'm sure she'll be okay."

"Right, well, let's ask her."

Artie perked up to be more like his old self, and I knew we were on the right track for once.

We went back to find Joy bustling around, and Gaby with her feet up. Artie spoke softly to Gaby alone, while I chatted to Joy. She was quite guarded at first, but after a few minutes, she started to tell me a bit about her life. It transpired that Joy had fled from a broken relationship in her little village. She had been badly hurt, and now, she couldn't show her face there. She was now quite open with me, and it felt as though she had been dying to talk but hadn't had the right listener.

"You're a doctor, aren't you?" she asked.

"Yes, doesn't make me any the wiser though!" I grinned.

"I've never told anyone this, not even Gaby. You promise to keep it confidential – aren't doctors supposed to do that?"

"Yes, of course."

"Joy isn't my first name; it's Lucinda. My family only called me 'Joy' because they said that's what I brought them, lots of joy. But I let them down by falling in love with the wrong person."

"We can't always help who we fall in love with."

"No, you're right, I couldn't help it. I know that lots of people thought it was wrong, including my family."

"Yes, families can be the harshest critics, always know what's best, don't they?"

I smiled, but I could see the pain on Joy's face.

"Ronnie was lovely. So kind, made me feel I could do anything."

"What happened?"

"Ronnie was a girl. Veronica. She was strong and brave and didn't mind about what people said. But I couldn't bring myself to go against everything I'd ever been taught. I felt in my heart I could, but my head wouldn't let me. Ronnie gave me an ultimatum, tell the family or she would. So, I left her and I ran. I ran, and ran, and ended up here. I don't want to go back. I wrote to Ronnie and told her to leave it be. I'll stay here and look after Gaby – oh, don't worry, I don't have those sorts of feelings for her or anything. I just want to be useful and unseen. Perhaps these feelings for Ronnie will go away, in time."

I looked at Joy's forlorn face. She seemed so lost and yet so determined. I knew what prejudice was like and how it disrupted and destroyed lives. Everyone had to deal with it in his or her own way. Joy was running away, just like I had done. I hugged her close and felt a tear drop down onto my sleeve. I wasn't sure if it was hers or mine.

"You're doing a grand job here, Joy. Gaby really needs you, and Artie is so grateful. Look, we might be going a way for a while, Artie and I. We need to earn some money, but we'll be back every month or so. Do you think you can stay, for a few weeks, maybe months?"

"Oh, yes, I'd be so happy to! And I can help with the baby when it comes. Do you think Gaby will be all right about it? I don't want her to know, you know, about what I just told you?"

"I promise I will never tell a soul."

We need not have worried. Gaby was pragmatic about the arrangements and was more than happy for Artie to be in my company, even if it meant being parted for a while.

"Go on you great ape!" She grinned at Artie. "Joy and I will be fine, far less mess when you're not around!"

"Well, that's settled then. How about we seal it with a glass of beer?"

Artie went to the old refrigerator and produced three bottles of lager; Gaby, of course, was abstemious because of the pregnancy, but Joy joined in the toasts to a new future.

*

Ursula

November 1980

Somehow, I could not bring myself to get in contact with George. I knew from my colleagues that Artie had been up and down again and that he had sustained a nasty wound in an accident. Confidentiality was, perhaps, not all that is should be, although no names were mentioned. From the conversation, however, it was obvious who was being discussed. In fact, the colleague who had taken over Artie's care was a good friend and was trying to get me to contact George. She knew how I felt about him and took it upon herself to be a go-between of sorts, trying to help, I suppose.

My PhD was going well, and so was my pregnancy. I decided that whatever happened, I was going to keep the baby. This was likely to be my only chance of motherhood, and I felt sure I could cope, even on my own.

A letter arrived. It had been redirected on a number of occasions and had finally reached me in Bristol. I was not overly surprised that it had come from George. I read it to myself.

Dearest Ursula,

I know you will probably be surprised to hear from me after all these weeks. Surprised, angry, probably you'll tear this letter up, and I wouldn't blame you. I wanted to write and apologize for everything. For my father and my reaction to my father, and my cowardliness in not running after you that day. Believe me, I wanted to, but well, I didn't. I can't really explain other than I probably need to grow up a bit more. I'm sure you're nodding at this point. No doubt you moved on with your life, and I wish you every success in whatever you want to do. You'll be brilliant, I know.

I wanted to let you know that I'm going to Western Australia for a bit. I think I need the experience, and it pays well. I'm taking Artie, too, to try and get him some money and a start in the next phase of his life. His wife Gaby is pregnant, so he'll be coming back from time to time. I would love to see you and maybe try and explain in person. I leave on the 23rd.

You must know how I will always feel about you.

Yours truly,
George

I checked the calendar. It was the 24th, and I was too late. My only chance of contacting George now was through Gaby and Artie.

My emotions were in turmoil; I felt all the old feelings bubbling right back up again.

I decided to pay Gaby a visit straight away, perhaps as a start in the right direction. She must have thought I was an idiot, but I called Gaby on the phone that morning and asked if I could come and see her.

I arrived at the little house and was met by a delightful woman in an apron. The house was small but well-ordered, and little trinkets graced each of the surfaces in the small parlour.

The lady named Joy sat me down, and then Gaby waddled in. We both looked at each other and laughed.

"How many weeks are you?" Gaby asked me.

"Twenty-ish."

"Me too! About 22!"

And, of course, the ice was broken. We chatted over a cup of tea and compared pregnancy symptoms – it was good to talk to someone, and I felt at ease.

Gaby went on to tell me that Artie was coming back in a couple of weeks, but in the meantime, she gave me the address she had for him in Australia.

"Thank you, Gaby," I said, after supping her tea and munching her ginger biscuits, evidently good for morning sickness.

"You will write to George, won't you?" she urged.

"Yes, I will," I said and took the piece of paper with the details on it and placed it safely in my purse. I felt better and less isolated now, and perhaps I would have the strength to write to George after all.

16

George, December 1980

Nothing could have prepared me for the beauty of the landscape that I found myself driving through. I had finally landed in Perth and was setting off up the coast in the battered old utility truck that had been sent to pick us up. Artie sat in the back with our entire set of luggage, and we trundled along with the vibrant colours of the sunset as our backdrop. A large kangaroo bounded along parallel to us and then made off across a huge plain toward a distant forest. The coastal shrubs became thinner and thinner, and red sand became the mainstay of our road. Derek, our aboriginal driver, chatted merrily as he swung the "ute" this way and that.

"Stopping at this farm," he cried as we jolted up a stony driveway.

I couldn't see any buildings, and it was another 20 minutes before a large wood-built homestead came into view.

"Den, my brother, works here, and the missus said you should stop for some tucker first."

The hospitality was overwhelming and Artie, and I tucked into some delicious steaks washed down with plenty of the local brew.

"How'd yer like the roo, then?" asked Derek.

"Sorry?" I said.

"Roo, kang-i-roo. You've just eaten him."

"Good Lord!"

Artie was grinning

"Might take a while to get used to the local cuisine," he chortled

"Er, it was delicious," I said.

After a couple of hours of good-hearted banter, Artie and I were shown to a clean and tidy, although minimalist, bunkhouse.

We couldn't believe that we were finally here. It had been nearly a week since we had left Blighty with flight delays and a couple of stopovers en route. I had tried to contact Ursula before I left and was still sore inside, as if something were missing. I knew I had to get on with life, and I wanted to make sure Artie was on the right track. We had been promised good wages, mine much higher as a doctor, but Artie's was good, too. With any luck, he would be able to go home with a nice little nest egg. His security financially would help his security mentally.

Artie and I had had plenty of time to talk while on our journey. I learned a lot about his illness, which he called a condition rather than an illness, and his perspective on life. He truly believed there was an afterlife and that what happened here on this mortal Earth was only the preparation for better things to come. He believed we came down in human form more than once and that there was a plan. By whom or why, he wasn't sure. He believed we had existed in previous lives and that our purpose on Earth was to learn and grow from those past experiences.

He also told me more of what had happened to him that first time in a psychiatric hospital. It was cathartic for him to talk and enlightened me about how his mind had been working during his "manic" state. Intuitively, I had felt that the medication he had been given was a hammer to crack a walnut, but medical science was fairly clumsy when it came to psychiatric illness, and there was still a terrible taboo over it.

I began to learn more about prejudice from Artie's revelations. How the doctor on the ward at St Austin's had been one-dimensional in his outlook and seemed unable to deviate from his preconceived ideas of Artie as a "mental patient" rather than a human being. Clearly some of the nurses had been sympathetic, but the whole system was geared more to containment rather than comprehension and cure.

Way out here at one of the furthest corners of the Earth, it seemed weird now that Artie should have been incarcerated for his "condition." I did, however, realise that in his heightened state, Artie could have been a danger to himself. He agreed that his perception of being able to fly was, perhaps, a bit too farfetched. We laughed about it, and I felt a real connection with my brother. He had a type of wisdom that I didn't possess, in spite of my fancy medical degree. We all needed to learn humility and kindness, a lesson taught to us through Isaac, our lost little brother. Artie felt that Isaac was now guiding us and that this journey was part of our road to enlightenment. I preferred to think of it as a great opportunity and a chance to try to forget Ursula, although this was proving harder than I had anticipated.

The next morning, we set off for the mine and bade our host farewell. My first impression of Australia was a raw and vast land that didn't care who or what you were. Everyone got on together, rich or poor, black or white. It was later that I learned that not all aborigines were as well adapted as Den and Derek. As always, in a country's history, the government hadn't always been exemplary when it came to dealing with the indigenous population.

We drove on through the day, stopping only for a pasty and water at a remote café on the dusty road. Here, we filled up again with petrol.

Eventually, we rolled into the mining compound. Artie was greeted by a foreman and whisked off to the miners' bunkhouse. I was shown to a small but clean and tidy hut with a bedroom, shower, and a room with table and chairs.

"This 'ere's your office, doc," said Derek. "Everything should be 'ere. The nurse 'll be in in the morning to go over stuff."

"Thanks, Derek."

And with that Derek chortled his way out of the hut.

There was a fridge in the corner of the large room. Inside, there were some beers and also vials of injections.

In one of the cupboards, there was some basic equipment, the sort of things a GP in England might have, but also a locked cabinet that I presumed had medication, some intravenous bags, and surgical sets.

I went into the bedroom, which had a battered old leather armchair in one corner and a comfortable looking bed in the centre. I stripped off and went next door to the shower. It worked well enough, and I was amazed at the amount of red dust that appeared in the bottom of the tray.

Artie and I didn't see too much of each other over the next few days. The nurse duly arrived, a rotund, smiling lady with large forearms and an even larger heart. She arrived with a fresh cup of coffee and a large pastry, which she plonked down in front of me.

"Get this down yer," she said. "Gonna be a long day, doc."

Her name, inevitably, was Sheila, and she was a widow in her late forties. Her husband, I later discovered, had been killed in a mining accident. She thought of each of the miners as her own son and knew every one of the 300 men in the mining unit.

After a few hours of being briefed about how things worked, I suddenly heard the loud roar of an engine.

"Mick's here!" she yelled above the row. "Grab yer bag, doc!"

She pointed to a large black medical bag

"Mick'll take you out to the mine now."

To get there, we needed a helicopter. I was truly a flying doctor.

Sheila and I arrived at the site and went across to a tin roofed building where a small queue of men had gathered. I then proceeded to hold a clinic out there in the blazing sun.

There were various minor complaints: tickly coughs, infected minor wounds, abscesses, and lacerations.

After a few hours of antibiotics dispensed and wounds redressed by Sheila, the clinic was over. It transpired that the mining company also paid for local farmers and their families to utilize the medic's services, so there were a few children and women, too.

Sheila and I jumped back in the helicopter for the 10-minute ride home.

The next day, the clinic was held in my quarters in the large room with chairs. Miners who were unable to get to the mine were seen here. It transpired that there was a regular too-ing and fro-ing of miners from base camp to the mine. I also discovered that, occasionally, Mick would turn up and whisk me off to a homestead. Sometimes, it was a sick child, sometimes, an accident on one of the farms. Occasionally, I would have to sanction the flight of a patient to the nearest big hospital in Perth. A special aircrew would arrive and take the patient off once I was satisfied that they were stable. In those rare instances, I would put up an IV drip and sometimes accompany the patient.

Four weeks passed, and it was time for Artie to have his first long break.

He had thrived on the hard, physical work and was looking forward to going home to see Gaby. The last morning before he left was a particularly hot and sweltering day. In was the heart of summer, in January, and there hadn't been rain for weeks.

A siren rang out.

"What on Earth's that?" I asked Sheila.

"Crickey, it's the mine alarm! Could be a blow-out!"

Mick was suddenly at the door,

"Doc, need you, one of the shafts has collapsed and there are trapped men…"

"Artie," I cried automatically

"Yer bro's okay; he's helping, but we've got some poorly ones."

I jumped into the helicopter with Sheila and all the equipment she and I could carry. We whooshed up in a flurry of red dust and dipped starboard towards the mine.

As we set down, a couple of miners ran over to us, and the foreman beckoned toward the eastern part of the complex. There were a number of shafts in the mine, and it was the oldest eastern one that had collapsed. The foreman tried to explain the technicalities, but my main concern was the miners that could be trapped.

"Are there any still down there?" I asked.

"We think Dickson is still in there; the boys are looking now. But there's four blokes that need yer over here."

There was a concussion, broken leg, fractured ribs, and lots of cuts and bruises. Sheila and I set about doing the initial triage and patch up. The men were stoical and practical. There was no drama, just monosyllabic replies, and, "Thanks, doc."

We managed to get the concussion into the shade. Sheila was in charge of 15-minute neurological observations. The broken leg was splinted, a drip put up, and analgesia given. Mick radioed for the hospital to send an air ambulance for him.

The foreman then ran over to me.

"We've located Dickson! He's stuck down the shaft; his leg's trapped, and we can't get it free. Can you come?"

I grabbed my bag and ran over to the mineshaft. There was a cage open with two helmeted men covered in dust

"We'll have to go down, doc. I can't have yer down too long cos I'm not sure how stable this all is, but reckon we're okay for now. Boys have shored it up well."

We descended into a dusty hole with the lights burning brightly on our helmets. It was still murky, and everyone coughed from the dust-laden air.

After a couple of minutes, there was a screech of metal as the cage ground to a halt. We crawled along a passage to where the outline of a man could just be discerned. He was covered in thick grime, and his face was contorted in agony. I fumbled in my bag and brought out a needle, syringe, and some morphine.

"It's alright, Dickson. We'll help you now," said the foreman.

"Can't feel me left leg," he grimaced.

I tore off the top of his shirt and dug the needle into the thick deltoid muscle that protruded.

"This should help with the pain."

"Thanks, doc."

The creak of metal brought us all to attention.

"Look we've got to get him out of here. His leg is trapped under this rock, can't shift it. What do you think, doc?"

"Um, well I…"

"Can you amputate?" cried the foreman.

My mind raced. I hadn't done orthopedics for a couple of years, and nothing had prepared me for this scenario.

"Take it off," breathed Dickson. "I know it's the only way out and from the sound of that metal groaning, it'll need to be quick."

Soon I could tell from Dickson's breathing that the morphine had kicked in, and the pain was numbed. I shone the light onto one of the surgical packages that was in my bag. There was nothing I could use for an amputation.

"Have you got any hacksaws up there?" I asked the foreman.

"Plenty."

"Right find me a 20 cm one, scrub it clean and dowse it in surgical spirit – Sheila will have some, get her to wrap it as sterilely as she can and bring it back to me"

I crawled closer to Dickson and his semi-severed leg.

"How's it feel, Dickson?"

"Can't feel much, doc," he breathed. "Do what you have to."

"Okay. I'm going to examine the wound and clean you up as best I can. I've got some local anesthetic here, and I'll get of much of that into you as possible. I'll cut away the superficial tissues and try and stop the bleeding. Let's get a drip into you first, the fluid will make you feel better."

I gave an IV bag to one of the men to hold and managed to get a line into Dickson's bulky forearm. He had veins like train tracks. The man held the IV bag aloft, and it started to drip slowly into Dickson's vein.

Next, I looked at the leg. The knee was intact, but there was a huge boulder compressing his lower leg. I ripped open his trousers and began dowsing the area with saline from another IV bag. I rubbed the area with iodine and made what sterile field I could, given the grime and dust, and started injecting local anesthetic all around Dickson's lower leg. I took a clean scalpel and started dissecting down to the fractured bone. I had a few little mosquito clamps that I was able to attach to any large bleeding vessel. Blood was oozing everywhere, and I was mopping and pressing for all I was worth.

"Got it, doc!" A package wrapped in clean bandages was handed through to me. A large bag of swabs and dressings also came down. "Sheila thought you might need these as well."

"Thanks!"

I changed the surgical gloves that were covered in blood and unwrapped the saw. I gave Dickson a small shot of morphine through the IV, hoping I didn't suppress his respiration and kill him that way! I tied a light tourniquet above the wound site, then, with hands steadier than I had hoped possible, I took out the saw.

"This is going to hurt like hell. Hold him, boys!"

As if in a dream, I sawed at the bone of the tibia. The creaking and groaning of metal above us got louder.

"Hurry, doc," hissed the foreman.

Dickson had passed out. I sliced through tendons and periosteum and then sawed through what was left of the fibula. The stump came free in a stomach wrenching pop. It was pouring blood. I grabbed every pad and bandage that I could and almost sat on the stump to try and stem the flow. I wound acres of tape around my makeshift bandages.

"Right. Let's get him out of here!" Rocks started to fall behind the boulder and what remained of Dickson's leg and foot. "Quick!"

We half crawled, half pulled Dickson to the waiting cage, drip somehow still in situ, and got him into the lift. The mechanism heaved and whirred, and we came into daylight. As we emerged, a thunderous roar emanated from the shaft, which then completely collapsed sending a huge plume of dust into the air.

"Thanks, doc," said the foreman. "Good timing."

The hospital plane had arrived, and two figures emerged in paramedics' uniforms.

"We'll take him from here."

Dickson was strapped onto a gurney, and his stump and leg elevated. Within minutes, he was airborne and on his way to Perth.

"Reckon you could do with this, doc."

An ice-cold beer was thrust into my shaking hand. Artie came over grinning.

"Reckon you saved him, bro! You're a hero!"

But the other miners slapped me on the back and simply said, "Well done, doc," as though it was just another day at the office. I was doing my job. I just hoped Dickson would survive.

Artie had missed his flight home with all the drama, so he stayed back at base with me that evening. I began to sense a brittleness about him, which made me uneasy once again.

*

Artie
February 1981

I was just about holding it together. The horror of the mine collapsing made me constantly frightened. Every time I went down one of those shafts, I got sweaty and felt the walls closing in on me. I'd kept it under control before, but now, I couldn't sleep at night for feeling terrified. I knew I needed the job badly, as I needed money, and George was so happy for me. I couldn't bring myself to tell him about how I felt, and I was also ashamed.

But this was the last straw, and I could feel myself tipping. I tried to remember all the lessons I had learned from Dr. O'Donnelly, but my mind started to jump back to that awful mental ward. I got flashbacks that would leave me in a pool of sweat at night.

I knew George could sense it. He knew when my mind started to rev up. He was exhausted from his own stuff, and so I let him sleep, but my mind raced away again. It was no good, I had to talk to him, and soon.

"George, sorry, mate, but look, it's a sign. We have to stop these mines; they're dangerous. It was lucky no one was killed. They're making so much money out of it. They're taking the lion's share. We've got to stop them, George. It's criminal. They'll stop Father Christmas soon. We've got to cut the crap!" I said as slowly as my brain would let me, though I knew I was jabbering.

"Artie, Artie, it's okay. Look, I know what happened was very scary, but we're okay. The mining company is very good. They look after everyone," George tried to console me.

"Let's go, George, come on!"

"Artie, your mind is racing, isn't it? Slow down."

I could hear George, and with a gargantuan effort, I managed to slow my breathing and tensed and un-tensed my hands, a thing I'd learned from Dr. O'Donnelly's team.

"I think I might need something tonight," I said.

"Good man, yes, a small dose of olanzapine, 2.5mg perhaps..." said George.

"Yeah, that stuff. Slow down, breathe, slow down, breathe..."

"Yes, that's good, Artie," George kept saying.

"I hate it."

"What?"

"The feeling that I can't get out, underground. I don't think I can do it anymore."

"What do you mean?"

"I get panic attacks when I get into that cage. I can't do it again."

"Oh, Artie! Why didn't you say something before?"

"Sorry, bro, I thought it might pass. Now, I realize that even these sorts of things can be a trigger to my funny episodes. I know, I need to speak up."

"Take this."

George passed me a small white pill. Usually, my mind would scream *no! Don't take it! Its poison!* But this time, I knew deep down it would help. My mind raced again and thoughts of my Uncle Arthur started to bubble up. Somehow, I had become obsessed with the thought that I was his reincarnation, and among my other odd thoughts, he started to pop up to the top. I decided that I had to tell George while there was still time before the curtain came down completely.

*

George
February 1981

I gave Artie a small dose of olanzapine and went over to his bunk with him. We sat for an hour or so as his thoughts slowed, and he practiced his breathing and relaxation techniques. He told me of his thoughts about our uncle lost in the Great War.

"Look, I know the war record isn't complete, but it's very unlikely that he survived. He'd be nearly 80 by now, and I think we would have known," I said.

"I know it's weird, but it's the connections, you see. The purpose. Do you think you could help me find out? I keep thinking I could be him, and its freaking me out."

"Maybe when we get back, I could write some letters." I knew I was placating him, and it was unlikely I would be able to find out anything more, but I needed to let him know I understood. I changed the subject.

"We need to get you sorted here and off mining duty. Sleep now, and I'll talk to the foreman in the morning. See if we can't get you an above ground job. Reckon he owes me one."

We managed to persuade the foreman that Artie would be better off above ground. Luckily, there was plenty for him to do, and although the wages would reduce a bit, it was still more than enough.

Everyone was buzzing after the earlier dramatic events. The talk was of closing down the old part of the mine. The manager came in later in the day to address all of us. He paid great tribute to all the men and how they had dealt with the disaster. No one had lost their life, and many lessons had been learned. He said that Dickson was doing okay and had sent him a hamper from the company. He thanked me, too, but there was no glory or excess praise, just down-to-Earth gratitude.

Artie and I sat and talked that evening. He seemed more lucid, but I knew we had to be careful at this point. If Artie could learn to control his thoughts better, he stood a better chance of dealing with his condition.

"I could stay here," said Artie. "I could bring Gaby over when she's had the baby and start a new life."

I wasn't so convinced, as I now knew that running away wasn't always the answer.

"I think we shouldn't rush into anything, Artie. We still have family back home." I was still thinking of mother, but also of Ursula.

Artie was still due for his break after his four weeks of hard, relentless work, and he was taking his medication well; so after he had packed his small bag, I borrowed a "ute" to take him to the airport. I thought about what he had said about staying. It was tempting.

I had been thinking about what I was doing too. The job was exciting, exhilarating at times, but I was living in a bubble that couldn't last forever. I thought about what I was running from, the death of Isaac, my father, Ursula, a proper career in medicine in England. The heroism of being a mining doctor was great, but not fulfilling in the way I had hoped it might be, and I realised I had to face up to those things in my life that kept creeping back into my consciousness.

I made a plan in my head to go back, I'd accompany Artie on his next "shore leave" and made my mind up to face my father and Ursula.

I looked around at the Australian sunset, and even the glorious fading pinks and oranges couldn't tempt me to stay forever. For the first time in a while, I felt calm and happy.

I had a plan.

17

Ursula, February 1981

I had battled with myself for some time, but I knew I had to do this one thing. On a bleak morning when my clinic had finished, I took out pen and paper and started to write.

My dear George,

Thank you for your letter.

I apologize for not writing sooner, but you will understand when you read further, I do not know how I feel. I must be honest with you, when you left like that, I was confused and upset. I thought that you had worked through your relationship with your father and learned to ignore his scathing remarks. Perhaps it was true, that you were out of your mind to be with a black woman. But there is a much more pressing matter I really need to discuss with you in person. I understand from Gaby that Artie is coming home in a couple of weeks. Please, could you let me know when you are coming back so that we could meet? I know this sounds rather cold and believe me that is not how I want it to be.

Let me know as soon as you can.

Take care,
Ursula

I went over it again and again, and it did not sound any better. I took the address that Gaby had given me and penned an envelope. During my lunch break, I was able to escape the hospital for half an hour and wandered to the post office. There, I sighed, the letter had been sent. I decided to forget about it and continue with my work. There were deadlines and meetings to attend and there was the ever-nearing question of how I was going to explain my pregnancy. I determined that no one had to know or had any interest in my personal affairs. It felt very lonely. Was there someone I could talk to? As a psychiatrist, there were many supportive mechanisms and supervisions, but I did not want a clinical view.

I decided to visit the old pastor in my church, recognizing that I ran the risk of my parents finding out. How stupid I was! They would find out eventually. It was just a question of how I would tell them. Pastor Adiobe would listen, I knew.

After work that day, I put on the baggiest dress I could find and set off to the little house next door to the church where my family had worshipped as a child. Pastor Adiobe was in his seventies now, but I had never found him to be a pompous or opinionated man like some in the church. He was kindly and wise, and I had great respect for him.

I knocked tentatively at the door, and his wife opened it

"Ursula, Ursula, come in, my dear! We have not seen you for so long. Come and take some tea with us."

Pastor Adiobe appeared in the doorway of their modest little sitting room. Religious pictures and paraphernalia were on every wall and surface. He could sense my discomfort.

"Come, Ursula. I have a little work I need to do next door in the church, will you accompany me?"

His wife looked crossly at him and bustled off into the kitchen

"Be sure to bring her back for tea!" she cried.

Pastor Adiobe took me gently by the elbow, and we soon found ourselves sitting together at the back of the church.

"Forgive me, Ursula. I hope you were not too thirsty. I thought perhaps you needed to talk to me; it is so long since I have seen you."

"You are very kind," I said, "and, of course, absolutely right. I needed a friendly face and a sympathetic ear. I know who will judge me, and I know it won't be you."

"What troubles you?" He smiled.

"I am pregnant," I said.

"I see," he answered. His gaze never left mine, and I found myself telling him about George and what had happened.

"Do you love him?" Pastor Adiobe asked me.

I knew that was the question I needed to face, and I knew deep inside that the answer was yes. But I did not want to place myself in a vulnerable position, and I had an overwhelming fear of being rejected.

I told Pastor Adiobe how I felt.

"What do you wish of me?" he asked.

"I do not really know. I think just someone to listen and to know I am not alone."

"We are none of us alone unless we choose to be so," he said.

I thought for a moment, then said, "I have written to George. What do I do if he does not answer?"

"Have you told him about the baby?"

"Not yet, but I feel I should."

"Well, what will you do if he does not answer your letter?"

"I do not know, Pastor, part of me wants to run and hide, but part of me feels we never really had a chance to work out where we were going before the incident with his father."

"Time, time and love."

Easy words, I thought, *but so hard to fulfill.*

"You know you can come and talk to me whenever you need to."

Pastor Adiobe had not judged me or berated me. I was able to do that all for myself. He had given me a sounding board and a view of what he thought God was about. This was something I had neglected for some time, and I was grateful to him for being so understanding.

"Come now, we must take tea with my dear wife, or I shall be in the dog house tonight!"

As I left the church that evening, I felt resigned, but happier. I would see what time brought, and if there was no reply, I would deal with that, too.

Artie
March 1981

I left George and Australia behind. The plane took off into the clear sky and banked to the left on the beginning of its long flight path to Singapore and then London. I was able to see the amazing coastline of the west side of that vast country from my porthole. It made me feel so small and insignificant. I had a long journey ahead, and I felt in a strange mood as my mind started to sift through what had happened in my life. I knew I had never come to terms with being sectioned all those years ago. I felt a weight, almost physical, because of it. A failure, out of control, ashamed, but also frustrated that people couldn't understand me or where I was coming from.

I decided to write down some more of my memories and feelings, as it was helpful for me to try and piece things together from that strange part of my life. I thought back to my time in hospital and then to the time I had spent under Dr. O'Donnelly's care, when he'd encouraged me to write, even though sometimes the words made no sense.

"They will in time," I heard him say.

Dr. O'Donnelly transferred me to his unit after all the papers were signed. He was a bundle of energy, full of Irish charm, and was quick to let rip with his hearty laugh. His staff obviously adored him, and he had got a group of open minded, non-arrogant doctors and nurses. He had set up in a small wing of an old asylum outside of London, down in Kent. The wards were not locked, and there were plenty of staff on hand so that it didn't feel like they were over stretched or stressed.

The atmosphere on the ward could not have been more different to the one at St Austins. I remember I hated the ward doctor there, whereas on Dr. O'Donnolley's unit, there were only nice, kind staff. This was the sort of environment I had longed for, and I soon set about sitting with a doctor and explaining everything that was going on in my head. I realize now it must have been a stream of words making little or no sense, but the young doctor listened attentively and made loads of notes. The next day, the same doctor came and sought me out and started to talk to me about the notes he had written. I corrected some of the stuff he had written, and as he then read it back to me, I began to settle within myself.

Here is someone who understands, *I said to myself*.

I asked him if he agreed with all my theories about life and God and spirits and stuff.

He said that is was not his place to agree or disagree but asked my permission to describe my thoughts to his supervision group. He also asked if I would be prepared to talk to some of them. I immediately agreed and felt that I was being taken seriously for the first time, and at last, I was being treated with respect and dignity.

Days passed on that ward, and the routine of one to one sessions, group sessions, and shared activities started to sooth my racing mind. It seemed that we were all there to learn, doctors, nurses, and patients alike. They also tried new ways of helping with the various mental conditions that the patients were suffering from. There were gardening, woodwork, art, and music sessions for us, with staff joining in and chatting to us as we worked. These were all voluntary activities, and it was amazing how many patients attended. The patients were also encouraged to talk to one another and share experiences while the staff were there to be thoughtful facilitators and non-judgmental about our mental difficulties. These were all life lessons that could be applied in everyday situations, and I learned a lot from the patients as well as Dr O'Donnelly, who provided a strong and caring leadership.

We arrived in Singapore and trooped off the plane for a few hours until reboarding was called for London. Soon, we were airborne again, and in spite of my sleepiness, I still kept on jotting down stuff as it came into my head.

I had drifted off to sleep, pencil still in hand, when I was woken from my dreams by the announcement that we were 20 minutes to landing.

Joy was at the airport to meet me and reassured me that Gaby was fine, now 32 weeks pregnant, and we set off home. I stuffed all my notes into my rucksack, and I had a pocket full of cash and a little toy kangaroo, ready for my newborn child when he or she decided to arrive.

The few days I had with Gaby were lovely, and we sat and talked for hours about how our lives would be with a little one now to care for. I asked about Joy, and Gaby said that at some stage she would need to move on, but that she was staying and helping for now. It seemed to me to be a good solution all round. I realised that Joy had a story of her own, but that she would tell it to us if and when she was ready.

Days passed quickly, and within no time, I was back in the air heading out to Australia for another month's work. Gaby had told me about her visit from Ursula, and I felt a huge sadness for George. He liked to play the tough guy and look after everyone else, but I knew his heart was aching, and I hoped I could help him find a way back to Ursula. Not only was I going to be a father, but now an uncle too, it all seemed so strange.

My return flight was bumpy, and sometimes, I felt as if the plane would drop out of the sky, but my mind was better, more relaxed, as if I had got a lot off my chest just by writing stuff down.

Finally, we bounced into Perth airport, and I was mighty relieved to be on the ground again.

I arrived back at the mine and headed off to meet up with George. I found him in his clinic with Sheila seeing the last of the day's patients.

"G'day, young Artie!" Sheila yelled as soon as she saw me. "George is just dealing with a young abo from the town. Taking him rather a long time."

I heard raised voices and decided to go over to the clinic room. I didn't expect to see what awaited me there. George was seated at his desk with a young aborigine boy towering over him with a knife.

"Its okay, mate," I yelled to try and distract him, and the lad swung round to gaze at me. I recognized that look in his eyes, glazed and scared at the same time.

"What's troubling you mate?" I said without emotion

The lad swung back and pointed his knife at George.

"Medicine man says he's poisoning me," he said pointing the dangerous looking knife at my brother's throat.

"Look, it's okay, I'm not poisoning you. I'm giving you medicine to help your epilepsy," George said with a dry mouth.

"Medicine man says yer killing me, got to stop!"

"Hey, look young fella, just put the knife down, and we can talk about this, no one wants to hurt you, and you don't want to hurt anyone, do you?" I said in as calm a voice as I could muster. The boy was tall, but I was too, and stronger, I reckoned.

I managed to grab hold of the young man's wrist, and he dropped the knife. Next thing, I knew, he was sobbing on the floor. George got up shakily and went to kneel by him; I knelt on the other side.

"Look," George said gently "No one wants to hurt you, like Artie here said, but you can't go round threatening people with knives. I know it's difficult, and I know the medicine man doesn't trust Western medications, but we're only here to help. And you know your Mum wants you to have the medicine, she's really worried about you."

"I'm an aborigine, I can't be weak, gotta be strong."

"Look, mate," said Artie "I'm a big bloke like you, but I have to take medicine for my nerves sometimes."

"Really?"

"Yeah, and I didn't want to, believe me. But I finally listened to the doctors, and they gave me the right stuff, and now, I'm as fit as can be."

"Really?"

"Yes, mate, and I know it's hard, but Dr. George here will work with you to make sure you get the right stuff, too."

"That's right! Look, let's sit down and maybe you can start with a small dose, what do you say?"

The big gangly aborigine, slowly got to his feet and walked sheepishly back to the clinic while Sheila stood arms akimbo at the door

"Come on, you great galumph," she crowed, and the lad smiled.

"Thanks, Artie, that was great," George whispered.

"Glad to help."

Now, for once, I felt I wasn't competing with George. We could be equal brothers. It had taken me this long to realize I was just as good, and just as valuable. Thoughts of reincarnation and Uncle Arthur faded. I resolved that I would never know, but could live with the uncertainty. I told George to forget about chasing ghosts, and he seemed understandably relieved.

Days passed, and the mine settled down into its routine. I worked hard and saw George from time to time. It never seemed to be the right time, and I didn't find an opportunity to tell him that Gaby had met Ursula. It didn't seem my place to tell George that Ursula was pregnant. I could only presume it was George's baby, but I didn't know.

George worked hard, too, but I sensed a change in him, a restlessness and homesickness that was beginning to become apparent. Soon, it was time for another monthly visit home.

"Come with me," I said to George one evening. "You're due a break, and it's a long plane ride on my own! I'm not so keen on those thunderstorms over Singapore either!"

Sheila appeared at the door with a bunch of letters.

"One for you, Dr. George."

I thought I recognized the handwriting from the clinic

"You go and read your letter, mate."

I knew it was from Ursula, and so did George.

*

George
March 1981

I went back to my room and sat and stared at the letter. Royal mail had taken forever to get it to me, and I was convinced it had been via the North Pole or somewhere, clearly by sea. I decided to get a beer and opened the amber bottle slowly, still staring at the letter. The sun was slowly leaving the sky and darkness was descending over the west and over me. I was caught up in so many emotions, my instincts telling me to leave it, that it was over now. Anticipation, catching me again, my mind tumbling over a dozen scenarios; good news, bad news, final news. In the end, I opened the letter and read it. I felt the content was somewhat cryptic, and I sat back in my chair and sighed.

"She's pregnant, George."

Artie had silently entered the room and was standing in the doorway.

"What, why didn't you tell me?" I gasped.

"Not really my place, and Gaby told me that Ursula had written to you, I presumed that's what was in the letter…."

"She's not said, in the letter, I mean, just that she needs to talk to me…"

I could see Artie's puzzled look.

The phone's shrill ringing pierced the silence. I got up to answer, hoping it was a medical emergency to distract my aching head.

"You got Artie there with you? Urgent call from England for him"

"It's for you," I mumbled and handed Artie the phone.

"What! When? How long? Okay, okay… Yep – on my way."

"What is it?" I asked, seeing the terrified look on Artie's face.

"It's Gaby, they say she's gone into labour a few hours ago, but it's far too soon. They're concerned and think it might be good if I was there. Oh God, she can't lose it, not again!"

"Look, we'll get a flight back, there's one in a few hours, I'll come with you. We'll make it, don't worry."

And so, once more we were heading for the airport, Artie in a blind panic and me not knowing which way up I was. I wasn't going to run away again. Whatever awaited me back in England, I would face. I swore to myself that I would visit my father once we'd got Gaby sorted, but I wasn't sure I believed my own apparent bravery. And Ursula, yes, I'd see what she wanted to tell me, even if it wasn't what I wanted to hear.

The flight was long and arduous. I was trying to keep Artie sane, as well as myself. Finally, we landed and rushed to the hospital where Gaby had been admitted at 34 weeks pregnant. They had managed to stop the contractions, and the doctors and midwives were confident that the baby would be fine, even if it came early.

Artie was a little less agitated as we sat down to have a coffee.

"I need to find Ursula," I blurted.

"Yes, Gaby's got her new address somewhere. I'll go and ask her."

"Thanks, Artie!" I smiled. "I think it's time your big brother grew up."

"Not a moment too soon," he grinned.

*

It took a couple of weeks, but I finally found out where Ursula was staying in Bristol and made tracks to visit her as soon as I could. I didn't want to leave

Artie, but I thought he would be okay for a day or so. Gaby's contractions had stopped, and Artie's panic had subsided a little.

I hired a car and drove down the M4 towards Bristol. After a few wrong turns and some blue air, I drove into the little street in Redland where she had her flat. With trepidation and not a little anxiety, I knocked on Ursula's door.

It took a few minutes, but eventually, I heard the sound of the lock disengaging.

"Hello," she said quietly. "Come in, I am a bit slow, as you can see… I take it you got my letter," she added, a little curtly.

"Yes, your letter. Artie told me that you were… Expecting."

"Yes, George, it is yours, before you ask."

"Oh my God, that's, that's amazing! Look, I want to help; look, I've got money. Gosh is it really true, are you having our baby?" I was suddenly a blithering fool, unable to get my words out in a straight line.

"Yes, George, I am."

"Why didn't you tell me in the letter? Well, it doesn't matter! Its brilliant, fantastic, and, well, we can do whatever you want! I mean, should we get…"

"Slow down, George, I need time to…"

"Process," I said, my pressure of speech coming to a halt.

"I was not being childish, George. I just do not know where we are right now, and it is going to take some time to work out."

"Yes, of course, that's okay. Take as much time as you need, but let me help, whatever you decide. I never stopped thinking about you."

The phone rang and rather broke the moment. I hoped and prayed that Ursula and I could rekindle what we'd had before.

"It is actually for you, George, it is Artie."

Gaby had gone back into labour, and Artie was in melt down.

"Look, I've got to go back to London for a day or two, just till Gaby's sorted out. Could I come back and see you afterwards? When are you due?"

"In four weeks."

"What do you think?"

"Yes, that would be nice."

"Can I take you out somewhere?"

"No, I am not great at getting in a car! I will cook us something, just let me know when you are on your way, and I will tell you what to bring."

"I will!" I reached over and kissed her on the cheek. "You look amazing."

As I left, I could have sworn I heard sobbing.

I got out to the car but couldn't leave. I'd left her for far too long before, and now, she needed me. Artie would have to deal with the birth himself. There were plenty of doctors and nurses around, and I could visit once the baby was born.

I rang the bell.

A dewy-eyed Ursula opened the door, and I just hugged her there and then on the doorstep. We both sobbed into each other's shoulders. Not sure, and don't care what the neighbours thought.

We talked for hours, and I endeavoured to fill her in on what my life had been like without her. I told her of Australia, of the sun and the heat and the dust, of the heroic miners, and Dickson and his severed leg. I told her of kangaroos at dusk and roo steaks (at which she somewhat balked) and how, try as I might, I couldn't get her out of my mind. She was stuck right inside my cortex, and I had no wish to ever dislodge her!

Later that night, as we sat together on Ursula's sofa, she gave a little yelp.

"You okay?"

"Yes fine… I am just going to get up and walk around a little; I have a bit of cramp.

Oh goodness!" she cried.

"What is it?"

"My waters have broken!"

"But you're only 36 weeks! Where are your notes?"

"Over there on the sideboard, and there is a bag packed ready."

"I'm calling an ambulance now!" I gasped as I ran around like a headless chicken. When I looked round, Ursula was giggling.

"Not sure which one is going to be the child!"

I laughed, too, and we sat down, Ursula on a large towel, to wait for the ambulance.

Ursula's contractions started to come more frequently, and she reached for my hand each time. She breathed through each pain even though beads of sweat began to appear on her forehead. I felt useless and elated all at once.

We arrived at the maternity unit and were greeted by a jolly midwife who whisked us into a delivery suite and took all Ursula's details. She produced her file of notes and the midwife looked through.

"All seems fine, my dear, I see you're 37 years old. No mention here of an amniocentesis, to see if the baby had any problems."

"No, I did not want one." I looked at Ursula, and she smiled. " It will be what it will be," she said.

The midwife examined Ursula,

"Four cm dilated, very good. Let's get that monitor back on properly."

The baby's heartbeat traced higgledy lines on a large piece of paper.

As things progressed, more people popped in and out, offering pain relief to Ursula and cups of tea to me. All were declined, and after a few hours, Ursula's breathing started to change.

"I think she's ready to push!"

*

Our son was finally born. The paediatrician took him straight over to a warm resuscitation table, and placed an oxygen mask over his face. It was the longest minute of my life, broken by a rather piercing yelp from our infant son.

"He's fine," said the paediatrician, "hale and hearty in spite of coming a bit early. He'll be fine, just needs feeding!"

I beamed at Ursula, who was trying not to cry and laugh at the same time.

"Does he look alright, George?"

I went over to the paediatrician and was handed the small bundle, who looked pretty good to me. He was a little small at four weeks early, but I thought just as well he didn't come at full term otherwise he would have been enormous!

I carried him over to Ursula, and she gently placed him on her chest. He snorted and snuffled, and everyone could see what he was after.

"Off you go, Dad, and leave your son to feed and your wife to have her stitches," the midwife instructed.

I turned at grinned at Ursula. 'Wife"- I liked how that sounded!

Once outside, someone came up to me and passed me a note.

There had been a phone call for me from Artie. He wanted me to get back to London as soon as possible.

I went back to see my son and Ursula and explained the situation back up north.

"We are fine," Ursula said, "Just come back when you can."

This time, I knew it was all going to be all right, and I swore I'd return as soon as Gaby was out of danger.

"Your family is important, and anyway, Mum and Dad will be here soon," she said.

"And they will want to meet you, so hurry back!"

"I will," and I kissed my future wife and our precious son.

Gaby had been labouring for some time, and Artie was getting very stressed. When I arrived some four hours later, there was a lot of consternation in the room. I took one of the midwives aside, explaining I was the uncle.

"Tell him what's going on," Artie implored the nurse.

"I'm a doctor," I said, sounding rather banal. "What's happening?"

"She's been in labour for 24 hours, and she's not progressing. The baby's getting tired, lots of dips on the trace in the last 10 minutes. We've called for the consultant, but Gaby's probably going to need a Caesarian section."

18
Zak Goldstein, 1945-1972

I was very thrilled when Geo and Sally called their son Isaac. It had to have been after me, I thought. Perhaps I was too presumptuous. I was Sally's second cousin, and I had lost touch with her for a few years. I was at the wedding though, of Sally and Geo, that is. It was our side of the family that was Jewish, and I was the only one left. It was so nice of them to invite me.

I was a bit wobbly, even in those days. I was not very good in social situations. I mumbled and lost my words. But my wife looked after me. She was Sally's cousin, so I wasn't really blood related to Sally and Geo. But I was thrilled when I heard they had another son. We couldn't have children, but we had lots of cats, and my wife has named them all. I got confused, as they all look alike to me. We had 10.

My wife told me about the Down syndrome baby, but I wasn't ashamed for them. I knew what it was like, not to be "normal," to be thought of as inferior, to be looked down on, just because of your religion or race or genes.

I didn't ask to be Jewish, but I was proud of my family and our father the jeweler. And the rituals we had as children. We didn't bother anyone, and we kept ourselves to ourselves. But we lived in Germany at the wrong time, and we were taken by the regime. By the Nazis. We were put into camps and separated. I never knew where my mother and sister went.

It was the smell. The smell of rotting flesh and decay and excrement, it pervaded. I couldn't get rid of the smell.

They made my father take the gold out of people's teeth and melt it down and make jewelry for their women. I occasionally saw my father. He was one of the last ones to be transported to the gas chambers. I didn't go. It was a miracle. I don't understand why I was spared. I suspect I would have been in the next batch to be sent away, but the British came and let us out. I couldn't walk, and it took a long time for me to recover. I still shook, but I was fortunate to meet Anna, and she looked after me ever since. I was so sad to hear that Isaac had died. He had a very short life and, like me, knew the prejudice that people have for anything "different."

But I understand he was happy most of the time.

I wonder if they called him Isaac because he was different, like me?

I was found at the gates of Belsen in a pretty sorry state. The British soldiers stood and wept, vomited in the bushes, or just stared and lit up their cigarettes. The smell of their smoke was almost comforting. I remember a young soldier who literally picked me up in his arms. He couldn't look me in the face. I had sores on my head where I'd been shaved and my bones crunched as he held me. He took me to a makeshift hospital, where a kindly doctor examined me. After many months of trying to survive, I was eventually transported to a hospital in Alsace and slowly made my recovery. My mind was of course, destroyed, and it is still recovering, but my body came back to life with nourishing food and physiotherapy. I literally had to learn to walk again.

After a few months we were transferred to another hospital, and some of us prepared to make the trip to Israel. There was a new movement, Zionism, and many of my fellow sufferers wanted to make sure something like this never happened again. I was too tired.

I was always good at figures, and I tried to mend my brain by using it to count and measure. Count and measure. I was good at it, and soon, I found myself keeping the books for a little firm in Strasberg. I earned a small amount of money and found a hostel to stay in. The firm was doing quite well and had opened up a branch in London in Swiss cottage. I was asked to go across to help them set up their finances and so travelled by train and boat to reach the metropolis, the centre of the free world. I spoke a little broken English but read and read to try and improve.

During my stay there, I noticed one of the secretaries. She seemed sad and lonely.

A bit like myself, I thought.

One day, I bumped into her at the Lyons corner house where I took my frugal breakfast. Somehow, we started talking. She corrected my English and was keen to chat. It was the first time I had even admitted to being in Belsen, and I always wore long shirts to cover up my number. But, for some reason, I showed it to Anna. She told me that she had lost someone in the war as well. She had walked out with a young pilot for a few weeks, but he never returned. She later heard he had been shot down over Germany weeks before the end of the war. It seemed that everyone had been touched by that ghastly era of our lives.

It was snowing. I didn't like the cold, and I couldn't get warm. I stayed in bed in my hostel, unable to go to work. Two days passed, and I must have been in a delirium with influenza. When I came to, Anna was sitting by my bedside. I reached for my thick-rimmed glasses to make sure I wasn't hallucinating.

"We missed you at work," she said.

"How did you know where I was?"

"I'm a secretary!" She smiled. "I have access to personnel files. Your neighbour let me in"

"Gosh, isn't that breaking company rules?" I said.

"Don't worry, I won't get the sack, and anyway, I wanted to see if you had those figures that Mr. Jonas wanted."

"Oh, yes, of course! I'm sorry, I've been a bit under the weather."

"Well, I'm here to look after you now."

"Thank you," I said, amazed.

I looked around the dingy room, a small table, chest of drawers, and iron bed that I languished in. What could I offer this woman?

Anna brought me food and washed my clothes. She busied herself around the room. One day, she announced that this wasn't good enough and that there was a room in the flat she shared with a friend. I found my possessions and myself outside a large block of apartments in St John's Wood. I moved into the box room in the little flat that Anna shared with her friend.

I helped Anna and her friend with their finances, and soon, we were a merry threesome. Well, as merry as we could be. We had few pleasures but managed to go to the cinema once a fortnight. We didn't drink or smoke, and so our needs were simple. I would read in the evening and sit by the little gas fire while the girls would bustle around the flat, tidying, mending and sewing. Anna's friend got engaged, and before long, she was moving out. The room she shared with Anna was a little bigger than the box room that I used.

I had been given a raise at work, and the boss wanted me to stay on at the London branch, even possibly become a director. I mentioned to Anna that I could pay more and that perhaps we didn't need to get a new flat mate, and she could have a bit more space to herself.

"Well, look, if we're going to do that, don't you think we'd better get married?"

"Really? You'd marry me?" I said, shocked.

"Yes, of course, you ninny!"

I wasn't sure what a ninny was, but I was happy to be one.

We were married at the local Registry office in the summer, and Sally, Anna's cousin, was a witness. The day was humid and warm, and although the weather felt heavy and threatening, the rain decided to stay away. I remember Sally sitting next to me afterwards in the little snug in the local pub and asking so many questions about my time in the death camps. I told her slowly, over my glass of sparkling wine, and painfully. I was not used to alcohol, and I think it loosened my tongue. Not really wedding conversation, but she wanted to know. She was a sweet person and always thinking of others. She was softer than Anna, who had a brusque way about her. I know that was to conceal her lack of confidence.

We were happy together, Anna and I. Anna looked after me, and I worked for as long as I could. We got a kitten quite soon after we were married, and then one cat led to another. I knew they were a comfort to Anna, and some of them often curled up on my knee at night.

I tried not to think of my time in Belsen or what my life would have been like had there been no Nazis, no war. Everyone has his or her cross to bear.

That sounds wrong coming from a Jew. But it's true, and perhaps, we're all here to learn, learn the lessons, stop the hate, prejudice, intolerance. I didn't do much towards that, but Anna did by marrying me, and Sally did by bringing up Isaac on her own.

We lived in a little cottage in Wales. We retired there early on a good package from my firm, and we saved a lot by not having children and only cats.

I heard about Isaac's death last week and Anna wrote a long letter to Sally. I hoped she could find some comfort.

I hadn't done much with my life, and I had often suffered, but I was content. *Yes*, I thought, *he was probably named after me, Isaac Goldstein, Zac for short.*

*

George
March 30, 1981

I was floating on air. I had a map, a lifetime now planned. I was grateful to whatever omnipotent being or otherwise had enabled my life to finally have meaning and purpose. It wasn't saving the lives of others, it wasn't saving the world, it was knowing that my DNA had been passed on, and together with the person I had been fortunate to fall in love with, I was now responsible, yes responsible for a new life. I'd been protective towards Isaac, my dear little brother, and I had always wanted to keep him from harm, and he was my own flesh and blood; but this was so different and not something anyone one could explain; it just had to be experienced.

With my mind overflowing with joyous thoughts, I turned my attention back to Artie, and the next few perilous hours for him.

We were in the bustling maternity unit, and I knew Artie must have been feeling scared and excited at the same time. Anticipation, what would it bring? Laughter or tears, the stakes were now so high. At these sorts of moments, you almost wanted time to stop, fast forward a bit so you could know the outcome of events, and then let yourself be prepared for the result. We had to be ready for everything possible, and that was so difficult for Artie. I should have had more faith in him, I knew. A caesarian section was routine to these skilled doctors and nurses, but I knew that although it very rarely went wrong, it did sometimes go wrong, and it could just be our turn in that great wheel of fate.

We stood together, hardly breathing, and watched purposeful doctors and nurses go in and out through those swing doors. Artie wanted to go in too, but I thought it best that he didn't, so we both crossed the corridor to some unwelcoming plastic chairs and sat outside the theatre.

"So, you're a dad then," Artie made an effort at small talk, trying to pretend it was just another day, just an ordinary day, and I felt for him.

"Yes, its weird… and you're going to be one very soon!"

"I can't believe it; finally, it's all coming together."

I hoped he was right.

"How's Ursula doing?"

"Well, the baby was a bit early, like this one, but they're doing fine. Ursula looks so serene, a natural mum."

"She didn't need a caesarian then."

I paused, this wasn't a competition, but somehow it would have been comforting for Artie if I could have said "yes."

"No, she managed to pop him out."

"What are you going to call him?"

"Gosh, we haven't even thought yet. I'll have to discuss it with Ursula, but I like the name David. He's such a little chap, like in David and Goliath, and I think that Ursula's father is called David."

We sat for a few more moments, but Artie's mind was understandably elsewhere, and I didn't want to seem superior in any way. I decided to walk outside for a breath of fresh air. It was impossible not to appear as if I was gloating, and I'm sure Artie wanted to wipe the silly grin from my face although I think probably he was oblivious.

"I won't be long," I said to Artie.

As I walked from the theatre area, I saw an older man at the nurses' station. He was familiar, that hair and the slight drooping of once broad shoulders. I realised it was my father and I paused, and then stood still. There were so many emotions charging around in my head, but the main voice that I heard in my crowded mind's ear was that of Ursula's. I knew what she would have wanted. Reconciliation. My little son was going to need to meet his paternal grandfather at some stage, and my father was about to become a grandfather for the second time in one day without knowing it.

I walked calmly over to the reception area. I took a deep breath and words flowed.

"Hello, Father. Artie's in the delivery suite waiting for Gaby to have her Caesarian section. It's fine, I'm sure they're both okay. There's something I need to tell you though…"

My father stood still, rendered speechless. I took him by the arm and over to a well-used vending machine.

"Hot sweet tea," I said. "Nothing like it."

We sat, and I proceeded to tell him about Ursula and David.

"Your grandson is mixed race, father. He'll need all the love and support we can give him. I'm going to marry Ursula, so you will have to get used to it. I don't want to fight. You'll need time to process all this, I know. Well, there. I've said what I needed to. I'll take you back to Artie and, who knows, another grandson or granddaughter might have arrived!"

Having hardly drawn breath, I got up to leave.

"Wait, George. Look, I'm sorry; I know I was far too hasty with you and your young lady. I can't say it wasn't a shock, and I know times have changed and, well, I wasn't there for Isaac, not properly; but I'll be there for David."

"Thanks Dad," I said, having not addressed him thus for many years. He sensed the softening in my tone and looked down and smiled. "I'll have to make sure Ursula wants to call him David though!"

We walked back to where Artie was waiting, pacing the floor and looking strained.

"How long do you think George? Dad, what are you doing here?"

"I'm here to help, let me know what I can do. Your mother is fine and anxious for news. I'll go and phone her and tell her about… David?"

Artie and I exchanged glances.

"Good," I said.

As my father turned to go, a theatre nurse popped out of the delivery room.

"Mr. Galley, your son is here! Would you like to see him?"

All three of us turned around, but Dad hung back allowing Artie and I to go in first. We donned gowns and plastic shoes and hats and the nurse handed the baby to Artie. A youngish man in gown and gloves came across to us. He was the paediatrician in attendance.

"We're not 100 percent sure yet, but we think…"

There was a pause, and although there was noise all around us, there was a strange silence.

"He's got Down syndrome, hasn't he?" said Artie.

Artie's eyes were glistening as he looked down at his infant son. The tiny baby looked so like our brother when he had been a baby. My father stood in the background and heard the pronouncement. His eyes were shining too, and he made no attempt to leave.

"Yes, I think he has Down syndrome" the paediatrician agreed quietly, "it sometimes happens in younger women. He may be a mosaic…"

I started to explain what the doctor had meant by this, and my father listened intently, but Artie stopped me, holding his hand up gently while cradling his infant son.

"He's beautiful," my brother Arthur said in a calm and measured tone. "That's all that matters, and his name is Isaac."

CPSIA information can be obtained
at www.ICGtesting.com
Printed in the USA
LVHW081446151118
597256LV00031B/699/P